My Animal Treasury

This is a Parragon Book
First published in 2003

Parragon
Queen Street House
4 Queen Street
Bath BA1 1HE, UK

ISBN 1-40541-941-5

Printed in China

My Animal Treasury

p

Contents

Monkey Mayhem

Mickey and Maxine Monkey had finished their breakfast of Mango Munch. Now they were rushing off to play.

"Be careful!" called their mum. "And please DON'T make too much noise!"

"We won't!" the two mischievous monkeys promised, leaping across to the next tree.

"Wheeee," screeched Mickey, and "Wa-hoooo!" hollered Maxine.

The noise echoed through the whole jungle – Mickey and Maxine just didn't know how to be quiet!

Ka-thunk! Mickey landed on a branch. Ka-clunk! Maxine landed beside him. Ker-aack!

"Ooohh noooo!" the monkeys hollered as the branch snapped.

"Yi-i-i-kes!" they shrieked, as they went tumbling down. Ker-thumpp! The jungle shook as the two monkeys crashed to the ground.

"Yipppeeee!" the monkeys cheered, jumping up happily.

"That was so much FUN!" exclaimed Maxine. "Let's go and get Chico Chimp and see if he wants to do it, too!" And the two monkeys scrambled back up to the tree tops, bellowing, "HEY, CHICO! COME AND PLAY WITH US!" as they swung through the branches.

All over the jungle, animals shook their heads and covered their ears. Couldn't anyone keep those naughty, noisy monkeys quiet?

Chico Chimp arrived to play with his friends. The three of them were having a great time swinging, tumbling and bouncing together when suddenly they stopped short. Grandpa Gorilla was standing in their path, glaring at them angrily.

"Go away, you mischief-makers," he said. "You've given us all enough headaches today. My grandson Gulliver is fast asleep by the river and, if you wake him up, I will be very, very upset!"

"Sorry," whispered Maxine, looking down at the ground. Everyone in the jungle knew it was a big mistake to upset Grandpa Gorilla!

"We'll be quiet," they promised.

Mickey, Maxine and Chico didn't know what to do until Mickey said, "Let's climb the coconut palm tree. We can do that quietly."

"Okay," the others agreed half-heartedly.

"I suppose it's better than doing nothing," said Maxine.

From their perch among the coconuts, the three friends could see right over the jungle.

They saw Jerome Giraffe showing his son Jeremy how to choose the juiciest, most tender leaves on a tree… and they saw Portia Parrot giving her daughter Penelope her first flying lesson. And right down below them, they saw little Gulliver Gorilla sleeping contentedly in the tall grass beside the river.

And – uh-oh! They saw something else, too… Claudia Crocodile was in the river. She was grinning and snapping her big, sharp teeth – and heading straight for Gulliver!

The friends didn't think twice. Maxine shouted, "GET UP, GULLIVER! GET UP RIGHT NOOOOOOWW!"

Then Mickey and Chico began throwing coconuts at Claudia.

SMAACCCK! they went, on Claudia's hard crocodile head.

"OWW-WOOW!" moaned Claudia.

"What's going on here?" Grandpa Gorilla shouted up into the coconut tree. "I thought I told you three to keep quiet!"

All the noise woke Gulliver. The little gorilla sat up, looked around, and ran to his grandpa, who was hurrying towards the river.

When Grandpa saw Claudia he realised what had happened. "I am so glad you're safe!" he said, giving Gulliver a great big gorilla hug. The three monkeys came down from the tree.

"We're sorry we made so much noise," Chico said.

By this time all the gorillas had gathered around, and so had most of the other animals.

"What's going on?" squawked Portia Parrot.

"Yes, what's all the commotion about?" asked Jerome Giraffe.

"These three youngsters are heroes," said Grandpa. "They have saved my grandson from being eaten by Claudia Crocodile!"

"I think you all deserve a reward," said Grandpa. "And I think it should be…"

"Hurrah!" cheered all the other animals and then they held their breath in anticipation.

"…permission to be just as noisy as you like, whenever you like!" Grandpa Gorilla announced.

"YIPPEEE!" cheered Mickey, Maxine and Chico, in their loudest, screechiest voices. Their grins were almost as wide as the river.

"OH, NOOOOO!" all the other animals groaned together – but they were all smiling, too.

The Hare and the Tortoise

Hare was the most boastful animal in the whole forest. On this fine, sunny morning, he was trotting down the forest path singing, "I'm handsome and clever and the fastest hare ever! There's no one as splendid as me!"

Mole, Mouse and Squirrel watched him from the fallen log. "Hare is so annoying," said Mole. "Someone should find a way to stop him boasting all the time!"

"I'll get him to stop!" said Squirrel and he jumped on to the path right in front of Hare. "I'm as handsome as you are, Hare," he said. "Look at my big bushy tail."

"It's not as handsome as my fluffy white tail and my long silky ears!" boasted Hare.

"Well, I'm as clever as you are!" said Mouse, hurrying out to join them. "I can dig holes under trees and store enough nuts and seeds to last all winter!"

"That's nothing!" said Hare. "In winter, I can change my coat to white, so that I can hide in the snow!"

"Now, is there anyone who thinks they can run as *fast* as me?" said Hare to the animals, who had gathered round. "Who wants a race?" No one said anything! All the animals knew that Hare was *very fast* and no one thought they could beat him. "Ha!" exclaimed Hare. "That proves it! I'm the handsomest, the cleverest *and* the fastest."

"Excuse me," said a small voice.

"Yes?" said Hare, turning around.

"I will race you," said Tortoise.

"YOU?" said Hare, in amazement. "The slowest, clumsiest animal on four legs?"

"Yes," said Tortoise, quietly. "I will race you." The other animals gasped and Hare roared with laughter.

"Will you race me to the willow tree?" Hare asked Tortoise.

"Yes," said Tortoise.

"Will you race past the willow tree, to the stream?" asked Hare.

"Yes, I will," said Tortoise.

"Will you race past the willow tree, past the stream and all the way to the old oak tree?" asked Hare.

"Of course I will," said Tortoise.

"Fine," said Hare. "We'll start at nine o'clock in the morning! We'll meet here, at the big oak tree."

"All right," said Tortoise. The other animals ran off to tell their friends the news.

The next morning, everyone had turned out to watch the big race. Some were at the starting line and others were going to the finish, to see who would get there first.

Magpie called, "Ready, steady, GO!" And Tortoise and Hare were off! Hare shot past Tortoise and, when there was no one to show off for, he slowed down just a bit. He reached the willow tree and looked behind him – Tortoise was not in sight!

"It will take him ages just to catch me," Hare thought. "I don't need to hurry. I may as well stop and rest." He sat down under the willow tree and closed his eyes. In minutes, he was fast asleep.

Meanwhile, Tortoise just plodded on. He didn't try to go faster than he could, but he didn't stop, either. He just kept going, on and on and on. The sun climbed higher in the sky and Tortoise felt hot. But he still kept going. His stubby legs were beginning to ache, but he knew he mustn't stop. Hare kept snoring under the willow tree.

Some time later, Tortoise reached Hare. First of all, Tortoise thought he should wake Hare up. Then he changed his mind. "Hare is very clever," he told himself. "He must have a reason for sleeping. He would only be cross if I woke him!" So, Tortoise left Hare sleeping and went on his way, walking slowly towards the finish line.

THE HARE AND THE TORTOISE

Later that afternoon, as the sun began to sink and the air grew chilly, Hare awoke with a start. "The race!" he thought. "I have to finish the race!" He looked around to see if Tortoise was nearby. There was no sign of him. "Hah!" said Hare. "He still hasn't caught up with me. No need to hurry, then."

And he trotted towards the clearing, with a big grin on his face. When he neared the finish, Hare could hear cheers and clapping. "They must be able to see me coming," he thought. But, as he got closer, he saw the real reason for all the noise and his heart sank. There was Tortoise, crossing the line. Tortoise had won! The animals were cheering wildly. As Hare crept up to the finishing line, the cheers turned to laughter. His ears turned bright red and drooped with embarrassment. Hare moped off and everyone gathered round to congratulate Tortoise, who looked shy, but very proud. He had proved that slow but steady always wins the race.

Somehow the animals knew that they wouldn't have to listen to Hare's loud, annoying boasting any more!

The Naughty Kitten

Ginger was a naughty little kitten. He didn't always mean to be naughty, but somehow things just turned out that way.

"You really should be more careful," warned Mummy. But Ginger was too busy getting into trouble to listen.

One day, Ginger was in a particularly playful mood. First, he tried to play tag with his smallest sister – and chased her right up an old apple tree. It took Daddy all morning to get her down.

Then, Ginger dropped cream all over the dog's tail. The dog whirled round and round as he tried to lick it off. He got so dizzy that he fell right over. That really made Ginger laugh until his sides hurt.

After that, Ginger thought it would be fun to play hide-and-seek with the mice – and frightened them so much that they refused to come out of their hole for the rest of the day.

Then, Ginger crept up behind the rabbit and shouted, "HI!" The poor rabbit was so surprised that he fell head-first into his breakfast. Ginger thought he looked ever so funny covered in lettuce leaves and carrots.

For his next trick, Ginger knocked over a wheelbarrow full of apples while he was trying to fly like a bird. He really couldn't help laughing when the apples knocked his little brother flying into the air.

And when one of the apples splashed into the garden pond, Ginger decided to go apple bobbing. How he laughed as the goldfish bumped into each other in their hurry to get out of his way.

Ginger laughed so much that, WHO-OO-AH! he began to lose his balance. He stopped laughing as he tried to stop himself falling into the pond. But, SPLASH! It was no good – he fell right in.

"Help! I can't swim," wailed Ginger, splashing wildly around. But he needn't have worried, the water only reached up to his knees.

"Yuck!" he moaned, squirting out a mouthful of water.

"Ha, ha, ha!" laughed the other kittens, who had come to see what the noise was about. And the dog and the rabbit soon joined in.

"You really should be more careful," said Mummy, trying not to smile.

"It's not funny," said Ginger. He gave the other animals a hard glare as Daddy pulled him out of the pond. But then he caught sight of his reflection in the water. He did look very funny. Soon he was laughing as loudly as the others.

After that, Ginger tried hard not to be quite so naughty. And do you know what? He even succeeded... some of the time!

A Hat
Like
That

Heather the cow took great care of her appearance. She had the shiniest hooves and the glossiest coat. She had already won three rosettes at the County Show, and she wanted to win more.

One windy afternoon, when Heather was standing near a hedge, she found a beautiful straw hat on a branch. It had a couple of holes in it, but an elegant cow has to put her ears somewhere!

She strolled back across the field with her nose in the air, and the hat placed firmly on her head. Heather couldn't wait to show it off to her friends.

But Poppy, Annabel and Emily simply carried on munching. Heather tried a tiny ladylike cough. The munching didn't stop for a second. So Heather coughed a little louder. The munching grew louder.

Heather couldn't bear it any longer. "Haven't you noticed it?" she mooed.

"Did I hear something?" asked Emily.

"It was me!" cried Heather, stamping her hoof crossly.

"Oh, so it was," said Annabel, and returned to a particularly juicy clump of green grass.

"Oh dear! I'm feeling rather sleepy, I think I'll just have a little snooze," said Poppy.

"And I'm going for a walk," said Emily.

Heather was not a patient cow. "Look at my hat!" she cried.

Of course, the other cows had noticed the hat, but they loved to tease their friend.

"I always think," said Poppy, "that hats are rather… old-fashioned."

"Nonsense," Heather replied. "Only the most fashionable cows are wearing them."

"It's new then, is it?" asked Annabel.

"Certainly!" Heather replied. "It's the very latest style."

"Didn't Mrs MacDonald have a hat like that a few years ago?" asked Emily.

"I don't think so!" Heather said firmly. "Mrs MacDonald is lovely, but she's not what you would call stylish. Only a prize-winning cow could carry off a hat like this."

"If you say so, dear," mooed Annabel.

That evening, the cows ambled into the farmyard to be milked. Before long, all the other animals had gathered round.

"They're admiring my hat!" whispered Heather to Poppy.

But the giggling and chuckling didn't sound as if they thought Heather looked beautiful. It sounded more like animals who thought she looked rather silly.

"Well, well! So that's what happened to Scarecrow Sam's hat!" cried Old MacDonald.

Nowadays, if Heather starts putting on airs and graces, Poppy, Emily and Annabel know just what to do – they start talking about hats, and Heather tiptoes away.

Desmond Grows Up

Desmond was the smallest monkey in the group. He couldn't wait to grow up. "Will you measure me?" he asked his friend Rodney. "I only measured you last Monday, and now it's Friday," said Rodney. "You won't have grown in four days!"

Rodney took him to the tallest tree in the jungle and made him stand with his back against it. Then he made a mark on the trunk at the top of Desmond's head. It was in the same place as the last mark.

"See," he said, "you are still the same size."

"Botheration!" said Desmond.

Later he spoke to his friend Bubbles. "Watch the top of my head," he said to her.

"Whatever for, Dethmond?" said Bubbles. She always called him Dethmond.

"Just watch," said Desmond. So Bubbles watched the top of his head.

"Well?" asked Desmond. "Well what?" replied Bubbles.

"Am I growing? Can you see me growing?" asked Desmond.

"No, of course not!" she said. "I knew it!" said Desmond. "I knew it! I'm never going to grow."

"Dethmond," said Bubbles, "you will grow! Honestly you will."

But Desmond was not so sure. "What can I do to get taller?" he asked Rodney. "Wait!" said Rodney. So Desmond stood next to Rodney... and waited. And waited. "You won't grow that fast!" laughed Rodney. "It will be ages before you grow up."

But Desmond didn't have ages. He wanted to collect coconuts... NOW! He tried to stretch. He asked all his friends to pull on his arms and legs and to squeeze him so that he would get thinner and taller. He hung from the branches of trees by his toes. Nothing worked!

Every day he watched as the other monkeys climbed the tall palm trees to pick coconuts and drop them to the ground.

One day, there was a competition to see who could collect the most coconuts. Rodney was the favourite to win. He climbed to the top and wriggled through the palm leaves, and then... oh dear... he got stuck!

"Help!" he called." I can't move." One of the other big monkeys went up to help, but he was too big to get through the leaves.

"Let me try," begged Desmond.

"OK," they said grudgingly. Desmond raced up the trunk. At the top he was small enough to reach his friend and help him to get free. Then he picked six or seven coconuts and dropped them to the ground.

When they climbed down the other monkeys crowded round to pat Desmond on the back.

"Wow!" said Bubbles. "No one has ever climbed a tree that fast before."

"Maybe you are all too big!" said Desmond happily. "I'm not in such a hurry to grow up after all!"

After that he didn't worry so much about being small, especially after he managed to collect more coconuts than anyone else, and won the competition!

Sports Day

The sun peeped over the higgledy-piggledy, messy alley. It was much too early to be awake – or was it? Lenny the kitten slowly opened his eyes and grinned – it was 'time-to-get-up' time.

"Get up, Sleepyhead!" he yelled to his twin sister, Lulu. "It's a great day for running and jumping." And he started to run round and round the dustbins.

"Okay, Lenny," yawned Lulu, still half asleep, "I'm coming."

"I'll race you to the end of the alley," cried Lenny.

"But you always win," moaned Lulu.

"That's because you're a big, podgy pussy," laughed Lenny.

Lulu giggled. "Cheeky kitty!" she cried. "Bet you can't catch me!" And she ran down the alley as fast as she could.

"That was fun!" cried Lenny, as he finally caught up with his sister. "What about some jumping now?"

"Great idea," purred Lulu.

So, huffing and puffing, the little kittens piled up some boxes and put a pole across the gap.

Lenny leapt over it first. "Whee!" he cried. "I bet I can jump higher than you!"

Suddenly, Lulu spotted a tatty old ball. "I bet I can throw it further than you!" she cried.

"No, you can't," cried Lenny. He picked up the ball and threw his best throw ever – but it hit Uncle Bertie right on the head!

Scampering down the alley as fast as they could go, the two kittens quickly hid behind a heap of old potato sacks before Uncle Bertie could spot them!

"Pooh!" said Lulu. "These sacks are really very smelly!"

Suddenly, Lenny had an idea…

Sticking his feet into one of the old potato sacks, he pulled it up to his tummy and began hopping and jumping around!

"Hey, what about a sack race?" he giggled.

Lenny hopped and skipped. Lulu wiggled and giggled.

"I'm winning!" squealed Lulu. "I'm winning!"

"No, you're not!" cried Lenny. He jumped his best jump ever – and knocked a huge pile of boxes over Cousin Archie!

"Uh-oh!" groaned Lenny. "Trouble time!"

Uncle Bertie and Cousin Archie were not happy. They stomped off to find Hattie, the kittens' mother.

"Those kittens of yours are so naughty," they complained. "You've got to do something about them!"

Hattie sighed. Then, spying two pairs of tiny ears peeping out from behind a watering can, she tip-toed over. "Time-to-come-out-time!" she boomed.

"What have you two been up to?" Hattie asked Lenny and Lulu.

"Running and jumping, Mummy," whined Lenny.

"We didn't mean to hurt anyone," whispered Lulu. But Hattie wasn't cross. She knew her kittens were only playing.

"I've got an idea," she said. "Why don't we have a sports day? We can all join in – there'll be plenty of running and jumping for everyone!"

Archie and Bertie didn't want to play – they wanted a cat nap!

"Okay," said Hattie. "We'll simply ask the dogs to join us instead."

So, later that day, Hattie explained her idea to the Alley Dogs, who all thought it sounded like great fun. And it wasn't long before Hattie had organised everyone and everything!

"We'll have lots of races," cried Lenny, excitedly, "running, skipping, leaping and jumping ones – perhaps a sack race!"

Suddenly, six pussy eyes peeped over the fence.

"Okay, everyone," cried Hattie. "Let's begin. Ready… steady… "

"Er, Hattie," asked Cousin Archie, popping out from behind the fence, "can I join in?"

"Us too?" cried Uncle Bertie and Auntie Lucy.

"Of course you can," laughed Hattie.

"Ready… steady… GO!"

Cousin Archie and Harvey raced up the alley and passed the winning line together. "Archie and Harvey are the winners!" cried Hattie. "Time for the sack race now!"

The dogs and cats all clambered into their sacks. But Lenny and Lulu began before Hattie could say "Go!"

"Hey!" cried Hattie. "Come back you two, that's cheating!" But it was too late. Everyone began leaping and jumping after the kittens.

"STOP!" shouted Hattie.

Lenny and Lulu stopped – but no one else did! They crashed into each other and fell in a big Alley Cat and Dog pickle!

Luckily, no one was hurt, but now they were all tired.

"Well, that was the best sports day ever!" said Harvey.

Hattie looked at the higgledy-piggledy mess.

"You're right," she laughed. "But tomorrow we're going to play another game. It's called tidy-up the alley!"

Suddenly, lots of barking and meowing filled the air. "Oh, no!" they groaned, and then they all laughed.

Gym Giraffe

Jeremy Giraffe loved going out with his dad to gather the juicy green leaves for their dinner.

"This is where the most delicious leaves are," said Dad, reaching w-a-a-a-y up to a very high branch. "Remember the tallest trees have the tastiest leaves, and the tiny top leaves are the tenderest!"

One morning, Jeremy decided it was time to gather leaves on his own. "The tallest trees have the tastiest leaves," he whispered to himself, "and the tiny top leaves are the tenderest."

Jeremy stopped at a very tall tree and looked up. There at the top were some tiny, tender, tasty-looking leaves. Str - e - e - e - etching his neck just as he had seen his dad do, Jeremy reached as high as he could. It wasn't very high! "Oh, no," he thought. "How will I reach the tiny, tasty top leaves if my neck won't stretch?"

So Jeremy went back home with his neck hanging down in despair.

"Why, Jeremy, what's wrong?" asked his mum. When Jeremy told her, she gave his neck a nuzzle. "Your neck's still growing," she assured him. "Eat your greens and get lots of sleep, and you'll soon be able to reach the tastiest, tenderest leaves on the tallest trees in the jungle!"

That afternoon, Jeremy went out to try again. Portia Parrot saw Jeremy struggling to reach the top of the tree. Trying to be helpful, she swooped down and plucked a few of the tenderest leaves for him.

When Portia gave Jeremy the leaves, his spots went pale with shame and embarrassment.

"I should be able to get those myself," he wailed. "Why won't my neck stretch?"

"Oh, Jeremy," said Portia, "your neck is just fine! Keep eating your greens and getting lots of sleep, and it will grow!"

"But I can't wait," Jeremy insisted. "Isn't there anything I can do to stretch my neck now?"

"Perhaps there is," said Portia, thoughtfully. "Follow me!"

Portia led Jeremy through the jungle to a clearing. Jeremy's eyes widened with wonder at what he saw. There was so much going on! Seymour Snake was wrapping himself round a fallen tree trunk. "Hello, Jeremy," he hissed. "Jussssst doing my sssssslithering exercisesssss!"

Emma, Ellen and Eric Elephant were hoisting logs. "Hi, Jeremy," they called. "This is our trunk-strengthening workout!"

In the river, Claudia Crocodile was breaking thick branches in half. "Just limbering up my jaw muscles," she snapped.

Leonard Lion was taking his cubs, Louis and Lisa, through their pouncing paces. "Welcome to the Jungle Gym!" he called.

A few minutes later, Grandpa Gorilla and Leonard Lion came to greet Jeremy.

"What can we do for you?" they asked.

"Can you help me stretch my neck?" asked Jeremy. "I want to be able to reach the tasty, tiny, tender leaves."

"You're still growing," said Leonard Lion. "You just have to eat your greens and get lots of sleep."

Jeremy's face fell, until Grandpa Gorilla said, "But we will help things along with some special neck-stretching exercises. Come with us!"

Grandpa got Jeremy started right away.

"S-t-r-e-t-c-h to the left! S-t-r-e-t-c-h to the right!" Grandpa Gorilla shouted. "Chin lifts next," said Leonard Lion.

Jeremy s-t-r-e-e-t-c-h-e-d his neck to reach the branch.

"Come on, you can do it!" Portia said, cheering him on. Grandpa Gorilla told Jeremy to lie down. Then he called Seymour Snake. "Start slithering!" he said.

"Aaaaakkkk!" gasped Jeremy, as Seymour wrapped himself round his neck. "Not so tight," said Grandpa.

"That's better!" said Jeremy, as Seymour slithered along, pu-u-u-l-l-ing his neck muscles. All the exercise made Jeremy hungry.

At supper, he had three BIG helpings of greens. He was tired, too, so he went to bed early and slept soundly.

Jeremy loved the Jungle Gym and couldn't wait to go back. After his workout each day, Jeremy ate a good supper.

"Exercising makes me soooo hungry…" he said, "…and soooo tired," he yawned, as he fell asleep.

GYM GIRAFFE

The next time Jeremy and his dad went out leaf-gathering together, Jeremy spotted some sweet-looking leaves right at the top of a tall tree.

"I'm going to get those," he said.

"They're so high up!" said Dad.

Jeremy didn't hear him. He was too busy stretching… and stretching… and stretching… until he stretched right up to the very top branch!

"I've done it, Dad!" he cried happily. "The exercises worked!"

"I don't think it matters," said his mum. "What matters is that you have a fine, strong, long neck that any giraffe would be proud of!"

"And I am!" said Jeremy, taking another mouthful of tasty, tender leaves. He chewed the leaves extra thoroughly — because he knew they had a very long way to go!

33

Cuddly's Jumper

Cuddly Sheep and Stout Pig were going to show the others how to knit. Cuddly Sheep was really good at knitting. But she needed her friend, Stout Pig, to help with the wool. Stout Pig couldn't knit, not even a little bit, but he was very good at spinning the wool for Cuddly to use.

Wool has to be made into yarn before you can knit with it. Yarn is made by twisting it, like string. That is what Stout did. He collected all the loose bits of wool that caught on thorny bushes around the farm and made long, beautiful lengths of yarn out of them. Then Cuddly used Stout Pig's yarn to knit lots of pretty things. She could knit woolly socks. She could knit woolly hats. She could knit the best woolly jumpers in the world!

Cuddly and Stout sat close to each other. Stout Pig sat with his back against a low hedge and Cuddly sat on the other side. The pig pulled out lengths of wool from a pile under the hedge. He started to spin the wool on his wheel, until it was twisted into yarn. Then he gave the end to Cuddly.

Cuddly made little loops of the wool and put them on two fat knitting needles. Then she started knitting.

"Knit one, purl one, knit two together," she whispered to herself. Only knitters know what these secret words mean. They must be magic words, because they are whispered over and over again.

"Knit one, purl one, knit two together."

The jumper quickly started to take shape. As it grew in size, the animals watching could see it was nearly all white, just like the colour of Cuddly's own woolly coat, with little bits in purple, like the berries on the hedge.

Stout had to work hard on the other side of the hedge to keep up with Cuddly Sheep.

Cuddly looked up. "Is it getting late? I'm getting a bit cold," she said. None of the others felt cold.

"You can put my blanket on," said Pebbles Horse. He pulled his blanket over Cuddly's shoulders. But Cuddly got colder. And colder!

"1 keep warm in the straw," said Saffron Cow. She covered Cuddly with straw. But the more Cuddly knitted, the colder she got.

And the hotter Stout became. Cuddly was trying to finish the jumper quickly before she froze. The faster she knitted, the faster Stout Pig had to turn the spinning wheel, and he was soon in a sweat!

Then the jumper was finished… and Cuddly was shivering! Her teeth were chattering! Pebbles looked hard at Stout.

"Where did the wool come from that you were spinning?" he asked.

"I used that bundle of wool under the hedge," said Stout. "It was here when I came."

Pebbles' large head followed the wool from the spinning wheel over the hedge. There was only Cuddly there. "Cuddly," said Pebbles '…I think you have been knitting your own wool!"

Cuddly jumped up in surprise. The blanket and the straw fell off. She was bare all around her middle. No wonder she was cold. Her wool was all gone.

"Oh well," said Cuddly Sheep, taking out the needles from her knitting. "Never mind! I have a nice thick new jumper to keep me warm!"

Barking Night

I t was the middle of the
night. Harvey and his gang
were fast asleep in the higgledy-piggledy, messy alley, dreaming of
yummy bones and chasing dustmen! The only sounds were the gentle
rumblings of Ruffle's tummy and Bonnie's snores!

Everyone and everything was fast asleep – or were they? Six naughty
Alley Cats peeped over the fence. They spied the snoozing dogs and,
grinning and sniggering, they scribbled and scrabbled up the fence.

"I've got an idea!" whispered Archie. "Listen… "

Wibbling and wobbling, the Alley Cats stood in a line along the top
of the fence…

"Those dippy dogs are in for a fright!" giggled Archie.

"I bet I'll be the loudest!"
boasted Lenny. The cats
took a deep breath, and
out came the scariest,
screechiest sounds you
ever heard!

The terrible noise woke
Harvey with a start and
made him fall off his
mattress, straight on to Mac!

"What's that noise?" yelped Mac. "Is it the bagpipe ghost?"

"G-Ghost?" cried Puddles, rushing up to Harvey. "Help!"

The noise made Patchy and Ruffles jump. They fell in a big heap on top of Ruffles' bed! "Save us!" they cried.

Harvey spotted the culprits. "Oh, it's just those pesky pussies," he groaned, "up to mischief us usual. Don't worry, everyone, let's just ignore them and go back to sleep."

But those naughty cats weren't finished yet!

"Look!" cried Lenny. "One of them is still asleep. We must try harder."

They were right – Bonnie was still snoring in her dustbin!

"Louder! Louder!" screeched Archie to the others. But could they wake Bonnie? Oh no! She just kept on snoring and snoring and snoring!

"Someone should teach those cats a lesson," growled Mac. "When I was a pup I'd…"

"Not now, Mac!" shouted the others.

Harvey smiled, he had an idea. The gang huddled together and listened as Harvey told them his idea.

"And me! And me!" cried Puddles, squeezing herself in.

The cats thought they were so clever. They laughed and then they wailed even louder than before!

Then suddenly, Lenny slipped and grabbed Lulu, who grabbed Hattie, who grabbed Bertie, who grabbed Lucy, who grabbed Archie – and they all tumbled headfirst into the pile of boxes and bins!

"Bravo!" woofed the dogs. "More! More!" The cats squealed and wailed and ran away. They'd had enough of playing tricks for one day!

"Now to get our own back," chuckled Harvey. The gang sneaked along the alley as quiet as little mice.

"Ready?" whispered Harvey. "Steady – GO!"

"WOOF! WOOF!"

The ground shook and the cats jumped high into the air.

"Ha-ha!" roared the dogs. "Scaredy-cats! Scaredy-cats! We've got our own back! I think that's enough frights for one night!" said Harvey.

"You're right," agreed Archie, sheepishly. "Let's go back to bed. No more tricks tonight."

Just then Bonnie woke up. "Is it 'time-to-get-up' time?" she asked, rubbing her eyes.

"No!" said Patchy, "it's 'time-for-bed' time!" and they all laughed and laughed.

"Oh, goody!" yawned Bonnie. "Bedtime! The best time of the day!"

"Oh, Bonnie," smiled Harvey. "What a sleepyhead you are!"

But Bonnie didn't care. With another enormous yawn and a stretch, she turned away and wandered back to her dustbin – she was *soooo* tired!

At last the cats and dogs of the higgledy-piggledy, messy alley snuggled down to sleep, dreaming of yummy bones and chasing dustbin men – and bowls of scrummy fish! The only sounds were the rumblings of Ruffles' tummy and Bonnie's snores.

Everyone and everything was fast asleep – or were they?

"TOOWHIT TOOWHOOOOOOoo!"

Such a Pickle!

Old MacDonald has quite a few pigs on his farm. He has two that are favourites – Percy, and the eldest one, Jonathan Jakes Jermington Jollop.

Jonathan Jakes Jermington Jollop is the pig's birth name, but now he is called something much less grand! This is the story of how he got his new name.

When Jonathan Jakes Jermington Jollop was a piglet, he somehow got the idea that he was much better than all the other animals that lived on the farm. It was partly because he had such a long name, and partly because Old MacDonald liked to come and chat to him.

"I don't know what's the matter with that young pig," clucked Henrietta the hen. "I said hello to him this morning, and he didn't say a word. He just put his nose in the air and trotted off."

"He did the very same to me," neighed Old George the horse.

Soon there wasn't an animal left on the farm who had a good word to say about Jonathan Jakes Jermington Jollop – and the piglet only had himself to blame!

So, when Jonathan Jakes Jermington Jollop saw Henry the cockerel standing on the henhouse roof, and he decided to climb on to the roof of his sty, that is why no one tried to stop him.

Now, pigs are not well-known for their climbing skills, but this didn't stop Jonathan Jakes Jermington Jollop! He scrabbled and scrambled, puffed and panted, and eventually the young pig found himself perched rather uncomfortably on the top of his sty.

He soon realised that he had a very big problem. Getting up had not been easy, but he could see that getting down was going to be practically impossible – and he discovered that he was scared of heights!

Before long, there was a crowd around the pigsty. There was mooing and baaing, neighing and clucking, as they looked at the panicking pig on the roof.

"How did that silly piglet get into such a pickle?" Annabel the cow mooed.

"What a ridiculous place for a piglet to sit," clucked Henrietta the hen. "That's a place for hens not piglets!"

"Hey, Pickle Piglet!" quacked Doris the duck. "What are you doing up there, and how are you going to get down?" she asked.

"I've been really silly," said Jonathan Jakes Jermington Jollop, looking very upset. "Please help me!"

With a laugh, Old George picked him up by his tail and plonked him on the floor.

Jonathan Jakes Jermington Jollop looked very relieved to have all four trotters on firm ground again, and he smiled happily at the other farm animals as they crowded round him.

Jonathan Jakes Jermington Jollop never put on airs and graces again, and no one let him forget his climbing adventure. From that day on, Jonathan Jakes Jermington Jollop was forever known as Pickles the pig!

On My

Own

Deep in the jungle, where only wild things go, Mungo's mum was teaching him what a young monkey needs to know. "Some things just aren't safe to try alone," she said.

"Why not?" said Mungo. "I'm big enough to do things – on my own!"

"Now Mungo," said Mum, "listen carefully, please. We're going to go through these trees. Stay close to me, and hold my hand. Did you hear what I said? Do you understand?"

"It's okay, Mum. I won't slip or fall. I can swing across there with no trouble at all," said Mungo. "I'm big enough to do it – on my own!"

And off he swung! "Hissss," hissed Snake, in a snake wail. "That pesky Mungo pulled my tail!" And did Mungo hear poor old Snake groan? No!

Mungo just laughed. "I told you I could do it on my own."

"Now, we're going to cross the river using these stones," said Mum. "But, Mungo, I'd rather you didn't do this alone."

"But Mum," said Mungo, and he ran on without stopping, "I'm really good at jumping and hopping. I'm big enough to do it – on my own!"

And off he sprang! "That Mungo trampled on my nose!" said Croc. "Next time, I'll nibble off his toes!" And did Mungo hear poor old Croc groan? No!

46

Mungo just smiled. "I told you I could do it on my own."

"Mungo," said Mum, with a serious look on her face, "the jungle can be a dangerous place. There are all sorts of corners for creatures to hide, so, from here on, make sure that you stay by my side."

"Oh, Mum," said Mungo, "I don't need to wait for you. I can easily find my own way through. I'm big enough to do it – on my own!"

Mungo thwacked Lion's nose as he sped past. "Ouch!" That Mungo's so careless!" Lion said. Did Mungo hear poor old Lion groan? No! Mungo just grinned. "I told you I could do it – on my own."

"I think I've had quite enough for one day," Mum said. "So off you go, little monkey! Now it really is time for bed!" It was Mungo's turn to let out a groan.

"I don't want to go to bed – on my own!"

"Don't worry," said Mum. "Come on, kiss me goodnight, and I promise I'll hold you and cuddle you tight."

Lion roared "Is that Mungo still awake?"

"Yes!" snapped Crocodile.

"Let's help him go to sleep," hissed Snake.

And into the velvety, starry sky drifted the sounds of a jungle lullaby.

Milly the Greedy Puppy

Milly the Labrador puppy just loved eating. She wasn't fussy about what she ate, and didn't really mind whom it belonged to.

"You'll get fat," warned Tom, the farm cat. But Milly was too busy chewing a tasty fishbone to take any notice.

One day, Milly was in a particularly greedy mood. Before breakfast she sneaked into the kitchen and ate Tom's biscuits. After a big breakfast of fresh sardines and milk, she took a short break before nibbling her way through the horse's oats. The horse didn't seem to mind.

Then Milly had a quick nap. She felt quite hungry when she awoke, so she ate all the tastiest titbits from the pigs' trough. But she made sure she left plenty of room for lunch.

After a light lunch, Milly couldn't help feeling just a bit hungry – so she wolfed down Farmer Jones's meat pie. He'd left it on the window ledge so he obviously didn't want it.

After that, Milly knocked over the dustbin and rifled through the kitchen waste. It was full of the yummiest leftovers.

There was just enough time for another nap before nipping into the milking shed for milking time. Milly always enjoyed lapping up the odd bucketful of fresh milk when Farmer Jones wasn't looking.

Dinner was Milly's favourite meal of the day. It was amazing how fast she could eat a huge bowl of meat and biscuits.

Before going to bed, Milly walked around the yard cleaning up the scraps the hens had left behind. Wasn't she a helpful puppy!

Just as Milly was chewing a particularly tasty bit of bread, she saw something black out of the corner of her eye. It was Tom the farm cat, out for his evening stroll. If there was one thing Milly liked doing best of all, it was eating Tom's dinner when he wasn't looking.

Milly raced across the yard, around the barn and through the cat flap.

"Woof! Woof!" yelped Milly. She was stuck half-way through the cat flap. Greedy Milly had eaten so much food that her tummy was too big to fit through.

"Ha! Ha!" laughed the farm animals, who thought it served Milly right for eating all their food.

"Oh, dear!" smiled Tom when he came back to see what all the noise was about. He caught hold of Milly's legs and tried pulling her out. Then he tried pushing her out. But it was no good – she was stuck.

All the farm animals joined in. They pulled and pulled, until, POP! Out flew Milly.

Poor Milly felt so silly that she never ate anyone else's food again – unless they offered, that is!

The Three Little Pigs

Once upon a time, there were three little pigs who lived with their mummy in a big stone house.

One day, Mummy Pig said, "Children, it's time for you to go out and find your fortune in the big wide world." So she packed a little bag of food and a drink for each of them, and sent them on their way.

"Goodbye!" she called, as the three little pigs set off on their adventure. "Good luck, my dears, and remember to watch out for the big, bad wolf!"

"We will, Mummy," called the little pigs as they waved goodbye.

After a while, the three little pigs stopped for a rest and decided that they should each build a house to live in. Just then, they saw a farmer coming along the road with a wagon full of golden straw.

"Please, sir," said the first little pig, "may I have some of your straw to build myself a house?"

"Yes, little pig," said the farmer, "of course you can."

So the first little pig built his house of straw. Soon it was finished. It looked very good indeed, and the first little pig was happy.

The other two little pigs set off on their journey together and, after a while, they met a man carrying a large bundle of sticks.

"Please, sir," said the second little pig, "may I have some of your sticks to build myself a house?"

"Yes, little pig," said the man, "of course you can."

So the second little pig built his house of sticks. Soon it was finished. It looked very good indeed, and the second little pig was happy.

The third little pig set off on his journey alone. He saw lots of people

with wagons of straw and bundles of sticks, but he did not stop until he met a man with a cart filled to the brim with bricks.

"Please, sir," said the third little pig, "may I have some bricks to build myself a house?"

"Yes, little pig," said the man, "of course you can."

So the third little pig built his house of bricks. Soon it was finished. It looked very good indeed. It was strong and solid,

and the third little pig was very, very pleased.

That evening, the big, bad wolf was walking along the road. He was very hungry and looking for something good to eat. He saw the first little pig's house of straw and looked in through the window.

"Yum, yum," he said to himself, licking his lips. "This little pig would make a most tasty dinner."

So, in his friendliest voice, the wolf called through the window, "Little pig, little pig, please let me in!"

But the first little pig remembered his mummy's warning, so he replied, "No, no, I won't let you in, not by the hair on my chinny-chin-chin!"

This made the wolf really angry. "Very well!" he roared. "I'll huff and I'll puff, and I'll blow your house down!"

The poor little pig was very afraid, but he still would not let the wolf in. So the wolf huffed… and he puffed… and he BLEW the straw house down.

Then the big, bad wolf chased the little pig and gobbled him up!

But the wolf was still hungry! He walked down the road and soon came to the house made of sticks. He looked through the window and called to the second little pig, "Little pig, little pig, please let me in."

"No, no!" cried the second little pig. "I won't let you in, not by the hair on my chinny-chin-chin!"

"Very well," cried the wolf. "Then I'll huff and I'll puff, and I'll blow your house down!"

And that's just what the big, bad wolf did. He huffed… and he puffed… and he BLEW the stick house down! Then he gobbled up the second little pig.

But the big, bad wolf was still hungry. So he walked down the road and soon came to the house made of bricks. He looked through the window and called to the third little pig, "Little pig, little pig, please let me in."

"No, no!" cried the third little pig. "I won't let you in, not by the hair on my chinny-chin-chin!"

"Very well," roared the big, bad wolf. "I'll huff and I'll puff, and I'll blow your house down!"

So the wolf huffed and he puffed... he HUFFED and he PUFFED... and he HUFFED and he PUFFED some more, but he could not blow the brick house down!

By now the big, bad wolf was very, very angry. He scrambled up onto the roof and began to climb down through the chimney.

But the third little pig was a clever little pig, and he had put a big pot of boiling water to bubble on the fire.

When the wolf came down the chimney, he landed – ker-splosh! – right in the middle of the pot of boiling water! He burned his bottom so badly that he ran out of the house and down the road just as fast as his legs could

carry him, howling so loudly with pain that he could be heard for miles.

The third little pig was very pleased with his house of bricks and lived in it for many years, happy and content. And nothing was ever heard of the big, bad wolf again.

Missing Mouse

In some ways, Molly Mouse was just like her brother and sisters. She had soft, pink ears and a cute, little nose. But, in other ways, she was very different…

Milly, Max and Baby Mouse were very tidy, but Molly was really, really messy! Her whiskers were never clean and her paws were always grubby. And, everywhere Molly went, she left a messy muddle behind her!

After breakfast, Milly and Max never forgot to make their beds. Each and every morning, they threw out their old bedding and made new beds with fresh, clean hay. But Molly wasn't bothered! She just jumped out of bed and left everything in a tangled, untidy heap!

"How can you sleep in that mess?" asked Milly, her sister.

At lunch time, the rest of the family nibbled their food carefully and always cleaned up after themselves. They brushed up their crumbs and cleared away their bowls. But Molly wasn't bothered! She just munched away merrily, scattering food everywhere!

"Why do you make such a mess?" asked Daddy Mouse.

At playtime, Milly and Max would carefully scamper up cornstalks. But Molly couldn't be bothered! She rushed up the stalks so fast, that she snapped them in two and fell to the ground in a messy heap!

"Why are you so clumsy?" asked Max.

And when Max and Milly collected nuts and seeds for their tea, they always stacked them in neat, little piles. But Molly couldn't be bothered! Her heaps always toppled over.

"Why are you so untidy?" asked Milly.

Everyone was really fed up with Molly and her messy ways. "Why can't you eat properly?" said Daddy Mouse.

"Why can't you keep yourself clean and tidy?" said Mummy Mouse.

"Why can't you be quieter?" said Baby Mouse.

"Oh, Molly," groaned Milly and Max.

"I can't do anything right," Molly sniffed. "It's not fair." And, with her messy tail in her paw, she said "Goodnight" and went to bed.

But Molly had a plan. She was fed up with all the grumbling and she wasn't going to put up with it any longer! So, when Max and Milly came to bed, Molly was already fast asleep – at least, that's what they thought. Molly was really wide awake!

She waited until her brother and sister were asleep and then crept out of bed. "No one loves me," she sighed. "I think I'll go and find somewhere else to live." So, off she set!

Molly had no idea where she was going. She scurried along the hedgerow and scampered through the cornstalks. And, as the sun began to rise, she slipped out of the field and happily skipped down the lane.

"I'll show them!" she said. "Why should I stay at home to be grumbled and moaned at? I'm going to find a home where people want me."

But, as the morning went on and Molly got further and further away from home, she became very tired. She sat down by a farmyard gate. "I'm really sleepy," she said and gave a big yawn! Then Molly noticed the barn door slightly open. Inside was a warm and comfy pile of hay – perfect for a little nap! She snuggled up in the hay and fell fast, fast asleep.

Back at home, when Mummy Mouse came to wake up her little ones, Molly's bed was empty. "Where's Molly?" she asked Milly and Max.

The two little mice rubbed their eyes and looked around. "We don't know," they said. "She was here last night, fast asleep."

"Daddy! Daddy! Come quick!" called Mummy Mouse. "Our Molly's missing!" So, they searched the house, but Molly was not there. They went outside and looked through the cornfield, combed the hedgerows, searched under and over toadstools, in fact, they didn't leave a leaf unturned! They even went down the lane.

Suddenly, Milly started jumping up and down. "Look!" she squealed, pointing at the muddy path that led into the farmyard.

There, right in front of Milly, was a set of tiny mouse footprints.

Milly and Max followed the footprints across the farmyard and into the barn. And there, fast asleep in a messy pile of hay, was Molly.

"We've found her!" they shouted.

Molly slowly opened her eyes. There were bits of straw sticking to her fur, her whiskers were crumpled and her paws were muddy. "Oh, Molly!" yelled Milly and Max. "We've missed you so much."

"How can you have missed *me?*" said Molly. "I'm always such a mess!"

"You might be messy," said her mummy, "but we love you just the same!" Everyone cheered and Molly smiled – they really did love her!

And with that, they set off home.

Copycat Max

Max was a little tiger with a bad habit. He was a terrible copycat! He copied everyone and everything. When the parrot said, "Pretty Polly, Pretty Polly," Max repeated it. "Pretty Polly, Pretty Polly!" Then, when the parrot got cross and said, "Shut up, Max, shut up Max," he repeated that as well. It was very annoying.

One day, he set off to explore. "I shall copy everything I see," he said to himself. And that's when the trouble really started!

First, he met a stork standing on one leg.

"Why are you doing that?" asked Max.

"Because it's comfortable," said the stork.

"How long can you do it for?" asked Max.

"For ages!" said the stork. "Only birds can stand like this."

"Hmmm!" said Max, and lifted up one leg.

"Now lift up two more," said the stork. Max did, and fell in a heap on the ground. "Told you!" said the stork. Max picked himself up.

Exploring further, he met a brown chameleon sitting on a green leaf. The amazing thing about chameleons is that they can change colour when they want to. The chameleon saw Max and changed his colour to green, like the leaf! Max could no longer see him.

"Where have you gone?" asked Max, looking everywhere.

"I'm still here," said the chameleon. "Watch this," he added, and he jumped on to a red flower and turned... red!

"Watch this then," said Max, and he lay down on some grass. "Now I'm green," he said.

"You're not," said the chameleon. "Only chameleons can change colour."

"Hmmm!" said Max. He rolled over and over in some mud. "Look," he said, "now I'm brown." Then he rolled in some white feathers. The feathers stuck to the mud. "Look," he said, "now I'm all white!"

"It won't last," said the chameleon.

Max decided to set off for home. He passed the stork still standing on one leg. The stork didn't recognise him.

He arrived home late in the evening. His brothers and sisters were playing down by the river. They saw a white figure coming towards them.

"WOooo!" wailed Max, pretending to be a ghost. "I've come to get you!" The tiger cubs were so scared, they rushed into the river and started to swim to the other side.

"WOooo!" wailed Max and rushed in after them. Of course, as soon as Max got wet, the mud and feathers disappeared. When the others saw it was only Max they were really cross.

"You frightened us," they told him.

"It was only a joke," said Max.

They agreed to forgive him if he promised not to copy anything again.

"Oh, all right," said Max. And, for the moment, he meant it!

Trunk Trouble

Emma, Ellen and Eric Elephant had spent nearly all day at the river, splashing and sploshing in the cool, clear water and giving each other excellent elephant showers. But now it was nearly dinner time, and their rumbling tummies told them it was time to head for home.

First the little elephants had to dry themselves off. They made their way out to the clearing, and carefully dusted themselves with fine earth and sand. WHOOSH! WHOOSH! PUFFLE! went Ellen and Emma with their trunks. Both sisters had long, graceful trunks, and they were very proud of them. WHOOSH! PUFFLE! WHOOSH PUFF! went Eric, when his sisters' backs were turned. COUGH! COUGH! AH-CHOO! went Emma and Ellen. "Hey! Cut it out!" they shouted.

Eric giggled – he loved annoying his sisters. "I'll race you home!" Eric called. "Last one back is an elephant egg!" as he loped off to the jungle.

Ellen and Emma ran after him. "We'll get there first! We'll beat you!" they cried, going as quickly as they could. Ellen and Emma were running so fast and trying so hard to catch up that they forgot to look where they were going. All at once, Emma's feet got caught in a vine, and she lost her balance.

"Oh-oh-OOOOHHHH!" she cried as she slipped and staggered.

"Grab my trunk!" Ellen cried, reaching out. But Emma grabbed her sister's trunk so hard that she pulled Ellen down with her and their trunks got twisted together in a great big tangle.

"Help!" they cried. "Eric! Help!" Their brother came bounding back.

"Don't worry!" he called. "I'll save you!" Eric reached out with his trunk to try to help his sisters up. But the vine leaves were very slippery, and, as he grabbed his sisters' trunks, he slipped and lost his balance, too. Now Eric's trunk was all tangled up with Emma's and Ellen's! The three elephants sat there in a sad, tangled heap. They could barely move.

"What are we going to do?" wailed Emma.

"Don't worry, someone will come and help us," Ellen said, hopefully.

"This is all your fault!" Eric grumbled. "If it wasn't for you two, I'd be home now, eating my dinner!"

A moment later, Seymour Snake came slithering by. "Isss thisss an interesting new game?" he hissed, looking at the heap of elephants.

"No!" sobbed Emma. "We're all tangled together and we can't get up. Can you help us, Seymour?"

"Well I'll ccccertainly do my besssssst," said Seymour. "Let's see if I can untwissst you." He wriggled in amongst the tangle of trunks to see what he could do.

But everything was so muddled and jumbled together that Seymour couldn't even find his way out! "GRACIOUSSS ME!" he exclaimed. "I SSSEEM TO BE SSSSTUCK!"

"Great!" said Eric. "Now we have a snake to worry about, too!"

"I ssssuggest you ssstart thinking about a ssssolution to all thissss," Seymour hissed. "I'm not too tangled up to give you a nasssty nip!"

Just then Mickey and Maxine Monkey swung through the branches.

"HEY, YOU GUYS!" they shouted. They weren't very far away – Mickey and Maxine always shouted. "WHAT'S GOING ON?"

"We're stuck!" cried Ellen. "Please untangle us so we can go home!"

"Well, we can try pulling you apart," said Maxine, scurrying down. "Mickey, you take a tail, and I'll take some ears."

Mickey grabbed hold of Eric's tail and Maxine gripped Ellen's ears. Then they both pulled and pulled and p-u-l-l-e-d.

"OUCH-OUCH-OOUUCCHH!" bellowed Ellen. "I'm being ssssqueezzzed breathlesssss!" hissed Seymour in alarm.

Mickey and Maxine gave up. Pulling clearly wasn't going to work.

Suddenly there was a flapping up above as Portia Parrot and her daughter Penelope flew above with something in their beaks. As everyone looked up, they let it go and a large cloud of dry, dusty, earth drifted downwards.

"Cough-cough-ca-choooo!" spluttered Mickey and Maxine.

"Cough-cough-ca-choooo!" thundered the elephants. At first, they didn't know what had happened. Then they realised – they had sneezed themselves apart!

"Thank you," cried the elephants and Seymour.

"Happy to help!" said Portia.

"Everyone's invited to our house for dinner!" said Eric.

"Hooray!" cried the others.

With their trunks held high, the elephants led the way – walking calmly and very, very carefully!

Birthday Surprise

In the higgledy-piggledy, messy alley, the sun was just beginning to shine. It was very early. Even the birds hadn't begun to chirp and cheep yet. Everyone and everything was fast asleep. Or were they?

Slowly, a sleepy head peeped out of a dustbin. It was Uncle Bertie.

First he opened one eye… then the other…and gave a great big grin!

"It's here, at last!" he chuckled to himself.

"Happy Birthday to me! Happy Birthday to me!" he sang, at the top of his voice. He looked around, but no one had heard. Everyone was still snoozing and snoring! Didn't they know it was his birthday?

"Time-to-get-up time!" he shouted, as he banged on a dustbin lid – CLANG! CLANG! CLANG! Lenny and Lulu, the two kittens, fell out of their basket in fright. Cousin Archie tumbled off his branch, right on top of poor Hattie!

"Uncle Bertie!" snapped Hattie, the kittens' mother, "why are you bashing that dustbin lid?"

"Sorry!" said Uncle Bertie. "Er… it's just that it's my… er… well, it's time-to-get-up time!"

"Oh, Bertie!" sighed Hattie. Now she was awake, she decided to get up and get her kittens ready. How they wriggled and wiggled—they hated wash time!

Cousin Archie scritched and scratched his claws on an old mat. Auntie Lucy just rolled over and went back to sleep! Poor Uncle Bertie! How sad he looked. Wasn't anyone going to wish him a happy birthday?

"Do you know what day it is today, Hattie?" he asked.

"Yes, Bertie," she replied.

"Is it a special day?" Bertie asked, hopefully.

"No, it's just a normal Tuesday," replied Hattie. "Now run along, I've got breakfast to make."

Then Bertie spotted the twins chasing a butterfly.

"Hey, you two!" he called. "Bet you don't know what day it is today."

"Of course we do," said Lulu. "It's Saturday!"

"It's not, Loony Lulu!" said Lenny and pushed his sister into a puddle!

"Oh, Lenny!" cried Lulu. "I'm telling Mummy!"

"No, twins," said Uncle Bertie, "it's my… "

But the naughty kittens were already halfway down the alley.

Suddenly, Archie jumped out from behind a box.

"Hello, Cousin Archie," said Bertie. "Bet you don't know what today is!"

"Bet I do," said Archie, with a grin.

"What is it then?" asked Bertie.

"I'm not telling!" giggled Archie and scampered off down the alley. "It's for me to know and you to find out!"

"But I do know!" cried Bertie. "It's my *birthday*!"

But Archie had already disappeared down the alley.

"I know who will remember!" said Bertie. "Harvey, the Alley Dog will – he knows everything!" And he rushed up the alley to find him.

"Hello, guys," called Bertie to the dogs. "Guess what today is."

"Snack day?" rumbled Ruffles, the Old English Sheepdog.

"Christmas day?" woofed Puddles, the puppy.

"No!" meowed Bertie, crossly. "Doesn't anyone know? It's... "

"Chasing Bertie day!" barked Harvey and started to chase him.

Bertie ran down the alley as fast as he could and jumped over the fence into the orchard.

"I don't care anyway!" he sulked. "Who wants a rotten old birthday?"

Poor Bertie didn't see the five pairs of cats' eyes peeping over the fence. And he didn't hear five pussies, planning and giggling!

"This is the worst birthday ever!" wailed Bertie.

"Tee-hee," whispered Cousin Archie. "It looks as though our plan is going to work!"

"I need to find the Alley Dogs," purred Hattie and clambered down from the fence.

Luckily, Harvey was already there!

"Is everything ready?" she asked. Harvey smiled and nodded his head.

Back in the orchard, Uncle Bertie was fed up. He decided to go home and have a sleep. He squeezed through a tiny gap in the fence and settled down under a tree.

"SURPRISE!" yelled the Alley Cats and Dogs. The alley was decorated with bright, colourful streamers. There was even a cake in the shape of a fish! Bertie was so happy!

"You remembered!" said Bertie.

"Oh, Bertie," said Hattie, "how could we forget?" She gave him a hug.

"Thanks, gang!" grinned Bertie. "This is the best birthday ever!"

Nibbling Neighbours

One sunny morning in the meadow, Annabel was happily munching away when she was surprised to discover a hole where there should be grass. "My dears," she mooed, "there's a hole in our field!"

There was no doubt about it. Someone had dug a round, deep hole in the ground.

"We must be careful not to fall into it," said Poppy, anxiously.

But the next morning, where there had been one hole before, now there were five! "If this goes on," said Poppy, "we'll have nowhere to stand at all!"

"And nothing to eat," added Emily, sounding alarmed.

By the end of the week,

there were over a hundred holes all over the meadow.

"You've got some nibbling neighbours," said Old MacDonald. "It looks like a family of rabbits has come to stay."

The cows shuddered. "Those hopping things with long ears?" asked Heather. "I can't look my best with them around!"

"And they have very, very large families," warned Emily. "Not just one baby at a time, like cows do."

"It's odd we've never seen one," said Poppy thoughtfully. "Maybe they do their digging in the dark. I'm going to keep watch tonight."

That night, as the full moon rose over the meadow, Poppy pretended to go to sleep.

Although she was expecting it, she was shocked when two bright little eyes and a twitchy nose popped up right in front of her.

"Aaaaaghh!" cried Poppy.

"Aaaaaghh!" cried the rabbit, and disappeared down its hole as fast as it had come.

"You should have followed it!"

cried Annabel, who had been woken by the sudden noises.

"Down a rabbit hole?" gasped Emily. "Don't be silly, Annabel. She's far too big!"

"Then we're doomed," said Heather, gloomily. "Those rabbits will take over without us even seeing them do it."

The next morning, the cows awoke to an amazing sight. Hundreds of rabbits were sitting all around them.

"Excuse me!" said the largest one. "We have come to ask for your help."

"Help?" echoed Annabel. "We're the ones who need help!"

The rabbit explained that his family lived in fear. "Your hooves are so big, you could stamp on us without noticing."

Just then, Poppy had one of her excellent ideas. "You would be much safer," she said, "if you lived under the hedgerow."

And they did. All day in the meadow, there's munching, mooing and mumbling. All night in the hedgerow, there's nibbling, digging and wiggling. And everyone is happy.

Tiger

Tales

Louis and Lisa Lion were just learning to pounce, and their dad had told them to practise as much as they could. So they were prowling through the jungle, looking for prey to pounce upon.

"There's something orange and blue and fluttery," whispered Lisa. "Here I go…" As Lisa pounced on the butterfly, Louis spotted something green and jumpy. He crept up and… POUNCED! As the two little cubs bounded through the jungle, Louis suddenly saw a flash of orange and black in some bushes.

"A stripey snake!" he whispered. "It's too good to pass up!" So, at just the right moment, he… POUNCED!

"Owwww!" came a voice from the bush. "What's got my tail?" The snake turned out to be attached to a stripey cub, just the same size as Louis and Lisa.

"Who are you?" they asked.

"I'm Timmy Tiger," said the little cub. "I've just moved here from The Other Side of the Jungle!"

"We're Louis and Lisa Lion," said Lisa. "Why don't we show you our side of the jungle?"

"Here's our river," said Louis proudly.

"It's nice," said Timmy, "but it's kind of small. Our river on The Other

Side of the Jungle is as wide as fifty tall palm trees laid end to end! And I can swim across that river – and back – without stopping once!"

"We can't even swim," said Lisa. "Will you show us how?"

"Err... maybe another time," said Timmy. "I'm just getting over the sniffles, and Mum said I shouldn't swim for a while."

A little farther along, Louis and Lisa saw Howard Hippo wallowing merrily in the mud.

"Meet our new friend, Timmy Tiger!" they called.

Howard opened his mouth in a big grin. "Nice to meet you!" he called.

"Er... same here," said Timmy, keeping his distance.

As the cubs scampered on, Timmy said, "On The Other Side of the Jungle, there's a hippo with a mouth as big as a cave. Three tigers can sit in it!"

As the cubs walked on, something from a branch above dropped down in front of them. Timmy jumped, but Louis and Lisa smiled. "Hi, Seymour! Meet our new friend, Timmy Tiger."

"Greetingsssss," hissed Seymour Snake. "Niccce to make your aquaintancccccce!"

"Nice to meet you, too," said Timmy, a little uncertainly. "Well, ssso long," said Seymour, as he slithered off. "Sssssee you ssssoon I suppose!"

As Seymour slithered off, Timmy said, "On The Other Side of the Jungle, there are snakes as thick as tree trunks. Once, one of them swallowed me!"

"Oh, no!" cried Louis and Lisa.

"Yes," Timmy said, "but my dad hit the snake on the head and made him spit me out! My dad's really, really strong, and he's twice as big as an elephant, and he can carry six gorillas on his back! And my mum can stand on her front paws and juggle coconuts with her hind legs, and… "

"…and what?" asked two smiling, normal-sized tigers on the path in front of them.

"…and, here they are," said Timmy, sheepishly. "Mum and Dad, meet my friends, Louis and Lisa."

"Happy to meet you," said Mr and Mrs Tiger.

"As you can see," Mrs Tiger added, "we are very ordinary and normal tigers."

"But what about all those amazing things Timmy told us?" asked Louis. "What about The Other Side of the Jungle?"

"It's just like this side," said Mr Tiger.

"So the river isn't as wide as fifty palm trees?" asked Lisa.

"And there's no hippo with a mouth as big as a cave, or a snake who swallowed Timmy?" asked Louis.

"No, indeed!" laughed Mrs Tiger. Timmy looked embarrassed. "Well, they were good stories," he said.

"Yes," said Mrs Tiger, "but they were just stories." She turned to Louis and Lisa. "Timmy had no friends to play with in our old home, he spent his time imagining amazing adventures."

"But now that he's got friends like you two to play with," said Mr Tiger, "perhaps he'll have some real adventures!"

"And there are more friends to meet, Timmy," Lisa said, "like Mickey and Maxine Monkey, and Chico Chimp!"

"You know, there are monkeys and chimps on The Other Side of the Jungle, too," said Timmy.

"Really?" said Lisa, glancing at her brother.

"Yes," said Timmy, "but I didn't know them. I can't wait to meet Mickey, Maxine and Chico!"

"Well, what are we waiting for?" said Louis, and they all raced off, ready for fun and excitement on This Side of the Jungle.

Sleepy the Farm Kitten

Sleepy, the farm kitten, was always tired. He liked nothing better than sleeping all day long, and all through the night. While all the other kittens were busy chasing mice or scaring away birds, he was normally fast asleep.

"Looks too much like hard work to me," he'd yawn, before strolling off to find a comfy spot for a snooze.

One day, while the other kittens were chasing mice around the corn shed, Sleepy stretched and looked around for somewhere to nap.

"You can't sleep here," said the farmer's wife, sweeping Sleepy out of the kitchen. "Today's cleaning day and you'll just be in the way."

"You can't sleep here," clucked the hens, flapping him out of the chicken run. "We're laying eggs and we certainly don't want you watching."

"You can't sleep here," mooed the cows, shooing him out of the milking shed. "We're busy being milked, and a kitten can never be trusted around milk."

"You can't sleep here," said the farmer, pushing him out of the dairy. "We're making ice cream and we don't want your hairs all over the place."

"I'm really tired," Sleepy complained to a passing mouse. "Can I sleep with you mice?"

"Don't be ridiculous," laughed the mouse. "Don't you know that kittens are supposed to chase mice?"

Just as Sleepy was about to give up hope of ever finding somewhere to sleep, he spotted the ideal bed – a soft bale of hay sitting on a trailer.

"Purrfect," he purred, curling into a sleepy ball. Within seconds, he was purring away in his sleep.

He was so comfortable, that he didn't even wake up when the tractor pulling the trailer chugged into life. And he still didn't wake up when the tractor and trailer bumped down the road leading to town.

It was only when the trailer shuddered to a halt that Sleepy woke with a start. He blinked his eyes sleepily, stretched, and looked around. Then he flew to his feet. He couldn't believe his eyes. He was at market and the farmer was driving away in the tractor.

"Wait for me," meowed Sleepy, leaping down from the trailer. But the farmer had gone. "Looks like I'll have to walk all the way home," moaned Sleepy, as he started to walk back towards the farm.

Sleepy walked all afternoon and all through the night. The cockerel was just beginning to crow the morning in when he eventually made it back to the farm.

"Hello, lazybones," called the other kittens when they saw him. "Where have you been sleeping all night while we've been chasing mice?"

But for once Sleepy really was tired – far too tired to explain where he had been all night. And it wasn't long before he was fast asleep!

Water Hunt

In the higgledy-piggledy, messy alley it was a very hot day. Harvey and his gang were melting!

"I need a slurpy, slippy ice lolly," sighed Ruffles.

"I need a cool pool to roll in," squeaked Puddles.

Those hot dogs just didn't know what to do!

"It's even too hot to sleep," complained Bonnie. "I'm the hottest dog in the whole world!"

"I bet I'm hotter than you!" snorted Ruffles.

"Oh no, you're not," replied Patchy. "I am!"

"I haven't been this hot," said Mac, "since I was in the desert when… "

"Not now, Mac!" the other dogs all yelled together.

"Stop!" cried Harvey. "It's much too hot to argue! Listen, I know what we'll do… "

"Let's play a game. Let's have a water hunt."

"Can I hunt, too?" yelped Puddles, hopping from one hot paw to the other.

"Do we have to move, Harvey?" groaned Patchy. "I don't think I can."

"Come on," said Harvey. "Where can we find some water?"

"I'm too hot to think," wailed Bonnie.

"We're too hot to do anything," said Patchy.

"Except eat yummy, cold ice cream," replied Ruffles, with a grin.

"I know," cried Mac suddenly. "Let's go to the seaside! We could play in the sand and splish and splash in the water."

"Good thinking, Mac," smiled Harvey. "But it's too far for us to go on a day like today. Can you think of something else?"

"I've got a *really* good idea – diggin'!" grinned Ruffles.

"Digging?" cried the others. "Dig for water in this heat?"

"No," said Ruffles excitedly. "Dig for bones. The dirt will be really damp and cool and we could roll around in it and... "

"No way, Ruffles," said Harvey firmly. "Today is not a digging day."

"Let's all go to the park," suggested Patchy. "We could jump in and out of the paddling pool and play in the fountain."

Poor Puddles looked as though she were going to burst into tears.

"But I can't walk that far, Harvey," she whispered. "I've only got little legs!"

"Don't worry, Puddles," said Harvey. "We wouldn't go without you."

"Oh, there *must* be some water somewhere!" Patchy puffed and panted.

"If I don't find water soon, I'm going to melt into a big, hairy puddle!" groaned Ruffles.

"Haven't you got *any* ideas at all, Harvey?" asked Mac.

But even Harvey was too hot to think, and Bonnie had given up and had gone to sleep in her dustbin!

Those poor hot dogs—what on earth could they do?

Meanwhile, the sizzling Alley Cats were searching, too. But they weren't on a water hunt. Oh no! They were on a mouse hunt— Archie had lost his favourite toy mouse!

"I WANT IT BACK!" wailed Archie, looking under a box.

"Well, it's not in here!" called Bertie from the top of a flower pot.

"Phew!" groaned Hattie. "It's way too hot for hunting, Archie. Why don't we have a cat nap instead?"

"Cat nap time!" said Lucy. "Great idea."

So the Alley Cats snuggled down for an afternoon nap – or did they?

Lenny and Lulu – the two little kittens – weren't quite ready for a nap just yet!

"Naps are for babies," whispered Lenny to his sister. "Come on, Lulu, follow me."

"Yippee!" giggled Lulu, "an adventure."

The kittens clambered and climbed over the pots and pans and headed towards a hole in the fence.

"Hey, Lulu!" cried Lenny. "I bet we find Archie's mouse through here."

So, carefully and quietly, the kittens squeezed themselves through the tiny gap…

Suddenly, a strange, stripey monster jumped out in front of them!

"AAAAAGH!" screamed Lulu. "What is it?"

Swooping and swaying through the spikey grass, the monster wiggled and wiggled towards them. Then it lifted up its head and gave a loud, angry "HISSSSS!"

"Oh no! It's a snake!" yelled Lenny. "Let's scarper."

Running as fast as they could, the kittens bounded towards a tree trunk and scampered up into its branches!

"We'll be safe up here," gasped Lenny.

But Lenny was wrong!

The sinister snake hissed louder and louder and slithered up the tree after them.

Lenny and Lulu quivered and quaked.

"HELP!" they wailed.

As the snake swayed about in front of the kittens, the poor little pussies began to cry.

With one, last enormous "HISSSSSSS!", the swinging snake leapt towards them – and got stuck in a branch!

Suddenly a great big spurt of water gushed from the snake's mouth, shot over the fence and into the alley below – SPLOOOSH!

Those silly scallywags. It wasn't a snake at all. It was a hosepipe and the cool refreshing water woke up Harvey and the gang – they couldn't believe their eyes!

"It's rainy and sunny at the same time," laughed Harvey.

He looked up and saw Lenny and Lulu peeping shyly over the fence.

"You clever cats," he called up to them.

"Three cheers for Lenny and Lulu!" cried the Alley Dogs. "HIP! HIP! HOORAY!"

And so, two cool cats had made five hot dogs very happy!

The Smiley Crocodile

Open-wide was the friendliest crocodile for miles around. While all the grumpy crocodiles were snapping and snarling and being very cross, Open-wide grinned at everyone. He had a very, very big smile.

"You smile too much," the others told him. "Be fierce… like a real crocodile!"

"I'll try," said Open-wide, and he put on a scowly face. It lasted two seconds and then the smile came back again. "How was that?" he asked. "Hopeless!" the others said.

One day, some hippos came to the river. They were very large and there were a lot of them. They waded into the part of the river that the crocodiles liked the best. Open-wide liked watching them having fun. He liked it when they sank to the bottom and then came up very slowly making lots of ripples. He liked it when they had a contest to see who could make the biggest splash. He liked it when they blew fountains of water up into the air. The grumpy crocodiles didn't like it one little bit!

"We'll soon get rid of them," they said. Open-wide saw a baby hippo playing in the water. His name was Sausage.

"I bet you can't do this!" said Sausage to Open-wide, and he blew a million bubbles so that they floated in a cloud across the top of the water.

"I bet I can," said Open-wide. And he did… through his nose!

"What about this?" said Sausage, and he turned on his back and sank below the surface. Open-wide did the same, and then he swam very fast to the opposite bank of the river. They played like this all day… and every day after that! Open-wide had never had such a good time.

The grumpy crocodiles were very fed up. They got together to think of ways of getting rid of the hippos. First they tried being frightening by showing lots of teeth. The hippos just smiled… and showed even bigger teeth! Then the grumpy crocodiles tried being rude.

"Scram!" they shouted… and, when that didn't work, "Smelly old hippos!" The hippos thought it was a joke.

Next they charged the hippos while they were swimming. The hippos sank to the bottom of the river where it was too deep for the crocodiles.

The crocodiles didn't know what else to do. Open-wide had an idea! "Why don't I just smile at them and ask nicely if they will move?" he said.

"Pooh!" said the crocodiles. "Fat lot of good that will do!"

Open-wide didn't give up. "Please?" "Oh, go on then," said the grumpy crocodiles, "but it won't work, you'll see."

But it did! The hippos liked Open-wide; he had a big smile just like them. They listened politely when he explained that the crocodiles didn't really like fun. They would rather be on their own and grumpy.

"We'll move further down the river if you will still come and play with Sausage," they said. And that's what happened.

The crocodiles were amazed! They didn't say anything to Open-wide, but secretly they wondered if smiling was better than scowling after all!

The Ant and the Grasshopper

Grasshopper was a lively, happy insect, who didn't have a care in the world. He spent the long summer days relaxing in the sunshine or bouncing and dancing through the grass. "Come and play!" he said to Bee one day.

"I'd love to," said Bee, "but I'm *much* too busy. If I don't gather this pollen, we bees won't be able to make honey. Then, when winter comes, we'll have nothing to eat."

"Well, work if you want to," said Grasshopper. "But *I'd* rather play!" And off he hopped. Then, Grasshopper saw Ladybird crawling along a leaf. "Come and play!" he called.

"Sorry, Grasshopper, not today," replied Ladybird. "I'm looking after the roses. They depend on us to guard them from greenfly!"

"Well, I think you're silly to spend this beautiful day working!" said Grasshopper, hopping away. Grasshopper went happily on his way, until he saw Ant, who was struggling to carry some grain on her back.

"Why are you working so hard?" asked Grasshopper. "It's such a sunny day! Come and play!"

"I have no time, Grasshopper," said Ant. "I have to take this grain back to my nest, so that my family and I have enough food when winter comes. Have you built your nest yet?"

"Nest?" laughed Grasshopper. "Who needs a nest when life in the great outdoors is so wonderful? And there's plenty of food – why should I worry?" And off he hopped.

At night, while the other insects slept, Grasshopper sang and danced under the moonlight. "Come and play!" he called to Spider, who was the only one awake.

"Sorry, Grasshopper," said Spider. "I have a web to spin. Can't stop now!"

"Suit yourself!" said Grasshopper, as he danced away. Day after day, Grasshopper played, while the other insects worked. And, night after night, he danced and sang while the others tried to sleep. The other insects were fed up.

"Stop that noise!" shouted Bee, one night. "You're keeping the whole hive awake!"

"Yes, be quiet!" said Ladybird.

As the summer went on, the long, sunny days began to get shorter and cooler. But lazy Grasshopper hardly noticed. He was still too busy enjoying himself. One day, Grasshopper saw Ant with her seven children. They were all carrying food back to their nest. "My, look at all your helpers," said Grasshopper.

"Well, we're running out of time," puffed Ant. "What are you doing about building a nest and storing food for the winter?"

"Oh, I can't be bothered," said Grasshopper. "There's lots of food around now, so why worry?"

That night, there was a chill in the air and Grasshopper didn't feel like dancing. "Maybe you'd better start getting ready for winter," warned Spider. It was getting colder, but Grasshopper didn't want to think about that now.

"There's still *loads* of time for that!" said Grasshopper and he began to sing.

Soon the trees began to lose their leaves. Grasshopper was spending more time looking for food, but there wasn't much food to be found. One afternoon, Ant and her children scurried across his path, each carrying a fat, ripe seed. "Where did you find those?" asked Grasshopper, eagerly. "Are there any more?"

"There are plenty over there," said Ant, pointing. "When are you going to make a nest? Winter will be here soon!"

"I'm too hungry to think about that now," said Grasshopper, rushing towards the seeds and gobbling down as many as he could.

A few days later, it began to snow. Ladybird was in her nest, fast asleep. Bee was in her hive, sipping sweet honey with her friends and relations. Grasshopper was cold and all alone. He was hungry and there wasn't a crumb of food to be found anywhere!

"I know," said Grasshopper. "Ant will help me. She has plenty of food." So he set out to look for Ant's nest. At last, Grasshopper found Ant's cosy nest, safe and warm beneath a rock.

Ant came out to see him. "What do you want?" she asked.

"Please, Ant," said Grasshopper, "have you any food to spare?"

Ant looked at him. "All summer long, while my family and I worked hard to gather food and prepare our nest, what did you do?"

"I played and had fun, of course," said Grasshopper. "That's what summer is for!"

"Well, you were wrong, weren't you," said Ant. "If you play all summer, then you must go hungry all winter."

"Yes," said Grasshopper, sadly, as a tiny tear fell from the corner of his eye. "I have learned my lesson now. I just hope it isn't too late!"

Ant's heart softened. "Okay, come on in," she said. "And I'll find some food for you." Grasshopper gratefully crawled into the warm nest, where Ant and her family shared their food with him.

By the time Spring came around, Grasshopper was fat and fit and ready to start building a nest of his very own!

Puppy's Paw

One sunny day, a small puppy sat in a grassy garden, watching Snowball and Snowdrop, his brother and sister, play. His coat was white with a few brown patches – and he had one brown paw. When he was born, his mummy said, "He looks like he's forgotten to put his other socks on! And that is how Socks got his name.

"Can I join in?" barked Socks.

"No, you can't!" Snowball yapped back.

"He looks like he's been having a mud bath, with those brown splodges," sneered Snowdrop. "Go and wash yourself properly, Socks."

"Maybe we should wash him," laughed Snowball. And the two puppies chased Socks towards the bird bath. Socks ran off as fast as he could and hid inside the shed – why didn't they like him? Was it because he didn't look like them? A big tear fell from his eye and trickled down his nose. Then, the two bouncy puppies appeared.

"Socks, where are you?" barked Snowdrop. Socks peeped out from behind the shed.

"We're going to the wood for a walk, Socks," called Snowball. "Bye-bye!"

Socks couldn't help himself. He ran out on to the lawn. "Please can I come?" he begged.

"You're much too young to come with us," said Snowdrop. "And you know Mummy says that you're too young to go out without her."

"I'm not too young," whined Socks. "I've been out loads of times."

"Well, you can't walk with us," said Snowball. "You must walk behind us."

"Okay," yapped Socks, eagerly. So, the two pups scampered through the garden gate, with Socks following. Snowball and Snowdrop ran down the lane towards the wood – Socks trotted behind!

In a clearing, there were two paths to choose from. Snowball's nose began to twitch. He could smell something wonderful. "This way!" he yelped and the two older pups rushed off.

"Don't those two ever stop to look where they're going?" wondered Socks, as he lifted his brown paw and followed. Round a bend, the puppies found a huge clump of beautiful, pink flowers. Socks pushed his soft, black nose into them. "Atishoo!" he sneezed, as yellow pollen flew into the air.

Snowdrop was busy chasing a butterfly. It fluttered away down another path and Snowdrop followed. "Come on, Socks!" barked Snowball. "Keep up!" and he set off after his sister.

"We'll get lost if we're not careful," thought Socks.

The butterfly led the puppies deeper and deeper into the wood. Suddenly, it flew high into the air and disappeared. Snowdrop and Snowball stopped and looked around. There were trees everywhere and they all looked the same!

"How are we going to find our way home now?" wailed Snowball.

"Listen," woofed Snowdrop. "There's someone through those trees. Let's see if they know the way home."

"I know the way…" began Socks. But Snowball and Snowdrop weren't listening. They had already dashed off along the path.

"It's easy," thought Socks to himself and set off after the others.

Tap-tap! Tap-tap! A woodpecker was trying to find some insects in a tree. "Can you help us find our way home?" asked Snowball and Snowdrop. But the woodpecker flew off!

"What are we going to do now?" whined Snowdrop. "I want my mummy!"

"Help!" they howled. "Help!"

"But I know the way home!" said Socks.

Snowdrop and Snowball turned to their brother and stared. "What did you say?" they asked.

PUPPY'S PAW

"I said I know the way home," said Socks, again.

"How?" asked Snowball.

"It's easy," said Socks. "Every time we chose a
path, we took the one on the
side of my brown paw. To get
home, we just turn round and take
the path on the side of my white paw.
Follow me and I'll show you."

So, back through the woods they went,
with Socks in front. Each time they had
to choose, Socks held up his brown paw,
turned his head and took the other path.
Back they scampered through the wood, past
the pink flowers, down the lane, through the gate
and into the garden, where their mummy was waiting for them.

"Where have you been?" she woofed, crossly. "I've been so worried."

"We got lost," said Snowball and Snowdrop. "It was all our fault."

"Socks was so clever," woofed Snowball.
"We're so lucky to have him as
a brother."

"I wish I had a brown paw like
him," said Snowdrop. "Do you
want to play ball, Socks?"

"Oh, yes please!" he
woofed, flicking the ball
across the lawn to his brother
and sister. Sometimes it was
good to be different!

Small and Pink

One morning, Percy the pig strutted proudly through the farmyard. "Today's the day," he told everyone he passed.

"What is he on about?" asked Doris the duck.

"Percy is expecting some piglets," clucked Jenny the hen.

"I didn't think boy pigs could have babies," said Doris, looking puzzled.

"No, no," Jenny clucked, flapping her wings. "They are coming from another farm to live here as part of his family."

Doris smiled. "Like Tilly and George and their new foal?" she said. "Oh, how lovely."

Percy had tripped and trotted from one end of the farmyard to the other more times than he cared to remember, but Old MacDonald still hadn't returned with the new arrivals.

Percy went back to his sty and checked it one more time. It was spotless. The straw was piled up neatly along one wall and the water trough was clean and full.

"I must make sure that everything is ready for my piglets," said Percy, brushing a speck of dust from the doorway.

Just as Percy finished cleaning, brushing and tidying he heard Old MacDonald's truck rumbling into the farmyard – they were here at last!

Percy was so excited! He hurried from his sty, but before he could reach the truck...

Whoosh! Something very small, very pink and very fast shot past his nose.

Whizzz! Something just as small and pink and even faster scuttled under his tail.

Wheeeee! Another small and pink and noisy thing zoomed straight under Percy's tummy.

"What's going on?" gasped Percy, as he spun round on his trotters.

"Eeeeeeeeee!" shrieked seven little piglets, dashing in every direction around the farmyard.

Late that night, a very tired Percy stood at the doorway of his sty – it was a tip. The straw was everywhere and the water trough was upside down. But seven little piglets were fast asleep in the corner.

"Tired, Percy?" asked Jenny the hen.

"Yes," sighed Percy.

"They never stand still from morning till night, do they?" added Maria the sheep.

"No," sighed Percy.

"Are you having second thoughts, Percy?" asked Old George the horse.

But Percy gave the kind of grin that only a very happy and contented proud pig can give. "Shhhhhhh!" he whispered. "My babies are sleeping!"

Hooray for Pepper!

Pepper was a very noisy puppy. He wasn't a bad puppy. He was just so happy that he barked all day long.

"Woof! Woof!" he barked at the cat, and she hissed and ran away.

"Woof! Woof!" he barked at the birds, and they flew up into the tree.

"Woof! Woof!" he barked at the tree, and it waved its branches angrily.

"Woof! Woof!" he barked at the postman, down the garden path

"Quiet, Pepper!" shouted Jimmy, Pepper's little boy. But Pepper just barked back cheerfully.

One day, Pepper had been barking so much that everyone was trying very hard to ignore him.

"Be quiet, Pepper," said Jimmy, as he lay down on the lawn. "I'm going to read my book and I can't concentrate if you keep barking."

Pepper tried his very best not to bark. He tried not to watch the butterflies and bees flitting about the garden. He tried to ignore the bright yellow ball lying on the path. And he tried extra hard not to bark at the birds flying high up in the sky. But, everywhere he looked, there were things to bark at, so he decided to stare at the blades of grass on the lawn instead.

As he stared at the grass, Pepper was sure that it began to move.

And as he carried on staring, Pepper was sure he could hear a strange slithering sound. He was just about to bark when he remembered Jimmy's words. He carried on staring. Now he could hear a hissing sound. Pepper stared more closely at the grass.

Pepper suddenly started to bark wildly.

"Woof! Woof!" he barked at the grass.

"Sshhh!" groaned Jimmy, as he turned the page of his book.

But Pepper didn't stop. He had spotted something long and slippery slithering across the lawn – something with a long tongue that hissed – and it was heading straight for Jimmy.

"Woof! Woof! WOOF!" barked Pepper.

"Quiet, Pepper!" called Jimmy's dad from the house.

But Pepper did not stop barking. Jimmy sat up, and looked around.

"Snake!" yelled Jimmy, pointing at the long slippery snake coming towards him.

Pepper carried on barking as Jimmy's dad raced across the lawn and scooped Jimmy up in his arms.

Later, after the man from the animal rescue centre had taken the snake away, Jimmy patted Pepper and gave him an extra special doggy treat.

"Hooray for Pepper!" laughed Jimmy. "Your barking really saved the day." That night, Pepper was even allowed to sleep on Jimmy's bed.

And, from that day on, Pepper decided that it was best if he kept his bark for special occasions!

Fancy Flying

Penelope Parrot and her mum, Portia, were having a wonderful afternoon, watching the Fancy Flying Display Team. Penelope could hardly believe her eyes as she saw the birds swoop and speed through the sky, doing their amazing tricks and wonderful stunts.

That night, Penelope dreamt about doing magnificent stunts with the other birds and, in the morning, she decided she would try to make her dream come true!

"I'm going to practise flying, Mum," she said. "I want to be the best!" Before Portia could say a word, Penelope had zoomed off.

"The first thing I have to do is learn to fly really fast," Penelope told herself. So she flapped her wings as hard as she could, to get up some speed. But Penelope had only just learned to fly – so she didn't know how fast or how far she could go. Soon she was huffing and puffing and panting, and her wings were flopping instead of flapping! "Oh, nooooo!" she cried, as she felt herself falling down... down... down... until... SPLASH! She landed right beside Howard Hippo, who had been enjoying his morning wallow. "Gracious, Penelope," said Howard, trying to shake the water out of his eyes and ears. "You must be more careful!"

"Sorry, Howard," said Penelope. "I didn't plan that. I was just seeing how fast I could fly and my wings got tired. I want to be a Fancy Flyer!"

"Then you'll need expert help," said Howard.

"But I don't know any experts," said Penelope.

"But I do," came a voice from the bank. It was her mum, Portia. "I've been trying to find you to tell you some special news," said her mum. "My uncle Percy has just arrived for a visit. He was a member of the original Fancy Flying team! He can give you the training you need."

Uncle Percy was delighted to hear that Penelope wanted to be a Fancy Flyer. "I'll teach you lots of stunts first," he said, "and then we'll work on one that will be your very own. Every Fancy Flyer has a speciality!"

Uncle Percy and Penelope went right out to start her training programme.

"We'll begin with the Twisting Take Off," Uncle Percy said. "Watch me and do as I do."

"Now, straighten up and fly forward!" Percy called. But Penelope couldn't stop spinning and spinning!

"Whoa!" she shouted. "I'm getting dizzy, Uncle Percy!"

Luckily, Penelope grabbed a branch and managed to stop spinning.

Jeremy Giraffe, who was nibbling leaves nearby, helped Penelope up as Uncle Percy flew back.

"Never mind," said Uncle Percy. "You'll soon get the hang of it."

Just then, Penelope's friends, Mickey, Maxine and Chico, came swinging by.

"Want to play Mango-Catch with us?" they called.

"Great!" said Penelope, flying over to join them.

"Wait!" said Uncle Percy. "A Fancy Flyer in training can't waste her energy on games!"

"Sorry, Uncle Percy," said Penelope. "I guess I'll see you all later," she said, a little sadly.

"In fact," said Uncle Percy, "I think it's time you were in your roost."

"But Uncle Percy," Penelope said, dismayed, "it's so early!"

"A Fancy Flyer needs her sleep, my dear!" said Uncle Percy. "Those wing muscles need lots of rest to prepare for all the work they must do."

"Better do what Uncle Percy says," said Portia, as she helped Penelope settle on to her bedtime branch. "He's the expert!"

The next morning, Uncle Percy woke Penelope up very early. "Time for your pre-dawn practice!" he squawked.

"But Uncle Percy, it's so early!" Penelope yawned. "The sun's not even up yet!"

"That's the best time to train!" said Uncle Percy. "Follow me!"

"We'll start with some speed exercises," Uncle Percy said. "This was my speciality when I was a Fancy Flyer. Just move in and out through the trees – like this!"

Penelope watched her uncle weave gracefully through the jungle. It looked easy, but when she tried...

THUH-WHACK! "Ouch!"cried Penelope.

Uncle Percy came rushing back to look at Penelope's head. "Nothing serious," he said. "A Fancy Flyer in training has to expect a few bumps and bruises! Best thing to do is keep going. Let's try it again."

All day, Uncle Percy tried to teach Penelope stunts. And all day, Penelope bashed... and crashed... and smashed... and splashed... into trees and other animals!

It was a very tired and worn-out Penelope who headed for home with Uncle Percy that afternoon.

"Well, Penelope," said Portia, when the two arrived back, "are you ready to be a Fancy Flyer?"

"Oh, yes," said Penelope. "And I know exactly what my speciality will be!"

"What?" asked Portia and Uncle Percy together.

"Watching from the audience!" laughed Penelope.

Little Lost Lenny

One grey day, Lenny, the kitten, was happily chasing his twin sister, Lulu, around the higgledy-piggledy, messy alley. They were having great fun, leaping over boxes and jumping through tyres.

Hattie, their mummy, looked up at the big, dark clouds. "I think we had better tidy up before it rains," she said. "Come on, everyone, let's put everything away."

So Uncle Bertie and Cousin Archie moved the boxes.

Auntie Lucy helped Hattie tidy away the blankets. Even little Lulu helped by clearing away her toys – she didn't want the rain to make them squelchy and soggy!

Everyone was busy helping… or were they?

That little mischief-maker, Lenny, was planning something naughty! He hid behind Lulu's dustbin, then leapt out and snatched her teddy.

With a giggle, he ran off down the alley. Lulu gave a long wail. Teddy was her favourite toy.

"Mummy!" she yelled. "Lenny's got my teddy!"

Lenny stopped at the bottom of the alley and called to his sister.

"If you want Teddy," he said, "come and get him."

Lulu raced down the alley.

Lenny giggled and tossed the teddy high into the sky.

He went straight over his sister's head and disappeared behind a large fence!

Lulu stood and wailed until all the other cats came charging down the alley.

Lenny knew he was going to be in big trouble.

"Whatever's the matter?" cried Hattie. The little kitten sobbed and told her mummy what her naughty brother had done to her teddy.

Everyone looked at Lenny.

"Lenny, you really are a naughty pussy!" said his mother, crossly. "You know you're not supposed to come down to this part of the alley."

Bertie scooped up Lulu. "Don't worry," he said, kindly. "Archie and I will find Teddy for you later."

Lenny stood still, bit his lip and trembled.

"Why do you have to get into so much trouble?" asked Hattie. "And why can't you be more helpful like your sister?" And off she stomped, back towards her dustbin.

"Sorry, Mummy," whispered Lenny.

A big, fat tear trickled down his cheek.

"It's not fair," he thought. "I didn't mean to lose silly old Teddy!"

Lenny gave a sniff and wandered over to the gate. He peeped through the rusty iron bars. Mummy had said that they must never, ever go through this gate.

"But I don't know why," thought Lenny.

"I do know that Teddy's in there, though," he said, "and I must try and get him back."

So he squeezed himself through the bars...

Lenny found himself standing at the edge of a big building site. There were wooden planks and piles of bricks everywhere – Lenny thought it looked great fun.

"I don't know why Mummy told me to keep away from here," he laughed. "It's like having my very own adventure playground."

The naughty pussy soon forgot about feeling sad as he climbed ladders and walked across gangplanks, high above the ground.

"I'm Lucky Lenny the Pirate!" he laughed. Then he stopped and peered through the rain.

"And there's Teddy!" he cried.

As Lenny grabbed the bear, the plank tipped up.

The rain had made it very slippery and... down, down, down he fell

– all the way to the bottom of a mucky, muddy hole.

Luckily, cats always land on their feet, so he wasn't hurt, but he'd had a real fright!

Lenny's little claws tried to grip the sides of the hole, but the rain had loosened the soil. It sprinkled down all over his head!

Oh dear, now he really was stuck!

"Mummy! Mummy!" he meowed. "Help! I'm stuck!"

Meanwhile, back in the alley, the cats were sheltering from the rain. Suddenly, Hattie looked round.

"Where's Lenny?" she asked, but no one had seen him for ages.

Hattie ran out into the alley. "Lenny!" she cried through the pouring rain. "Lenny, where are you?"

She knew something was wrong.

"Go and get the dogs," she said to Archie. "Ask them to help us find my poor, little Lenny."

Archie quickly returned with Harvey and the gang.

"Don't worry, Hattie," said Harvey. "We'll soon find him."

All the dogs and cats ran out into the pouring rain, meowing and barking Lenny's name.

At the bottom of the alley, the Old English Sheepdog, Ruffles, sniffed.

"I can smell him!" he yelped. "He's very near!" He snuffled to the gate.

"Yes, he's in there!" cried Patchy, the dog with a patch over one eye, "I can hear him crying!"

The animals rushed through the gate and quickly found the muddy hole where Lenny was stuck.

"Don't worry!" called Harvey. "We'll soon get you out."

Uncle Bertie found a thick rope. "We can use this," he called.

Ruffles, Harvey and Bertie lowered the rope to Lenny. The tiny kitten clung on tight and was pulled to safety. Lenny gave Teddy back to Lulu. "I didn't mean to make you sad," he said.

"We were so worried!" said Hattie. "No kitty treats for you tonight."

"I'm really sorry, Mummy," sniffed Lenny.

Hattie smiled and gave her naughty, little kitten a big hug. "That's okay," she smiled. "At least you're safe now."

Then, all the Alley Cats went back to the alley for lots of cat-napping!

Aunty and the Flowers

Every year on the farm, the animals had a competition. Everyone liked to join in the fun, and there was a prize for the winner. The prize could be for anything. One year, it was for growing the best purple vegetables. Once it was for having the knobbliest knees. (Gladys the duck won that, of course.)

This year they decided the prize would be for the best display of flowers. But who would choose the winner?

If Nelly the hen were the judge, she would make herself the winner. She always did. Bramble the sheep caught her wool on everything. She pulled the tables and chairs down behind her wherever she went.

Blink the pig covered everything in mud and Rambo the big horse couldn't even get into the tent!

But Aunty the goat wanted the job. She told the others how much she liked flowers. So why not? Aunty had never been a judge before and so she was chosen.

The big day came. Everyone had been busy for days. The tent was full of flowers, colour and light. Perfect!

The judge, Aunty, came in first. She looked very important and was taken to the first display made by Bramble the sheep.

"So I just choose which flowers I like best?" Aunty asked.

"Yes, we walk along the table, and whichever display you think is best wins the prize. This is Bramble's display. He has spent all morning getting it right," said Blink the pig.

"It's called 'Daisies and Dandelions'," said Bramble proudly. The flowers were white and yellow and looked very pretty in a blue mug. Aunty looked at them carefully. She sniffed them. And then she ate them.

The others were so surprised, that they couldn't speak! They just stared as Aunty went to the next one, "Buttercups and Roses". She ate them too!

The goat tilted her head back, half closed her eyes in a very thoughtful sort of way, and compared "Buttercups and Roses" with "Daisies and Dandelions".

Moving along the line, she ate "Cowslips and Honeysuckle". Then she ate "Chrysanthemums and Poppies". Aunty wrinkled up her nose.

"Bit sour, that," she said. She turned at last and saw all the others looking at her with their mouths open. She looked from one to the other, red poppies drooping from the sides of her mouth.

"What?" she said, puzzled. "What!"

Rambo said, "You were supposed to judge how pretty the flowers are!"

"Flowers are pretty as well?" asked Aunty.

Everyone burst out laughing. They had to explain it all to Aunty. She thought the whole idea of just looking at flowers was very odd.

There was no time to pick more flowers and start again. Instead, they gave Bramble the prize... Aunty had decided that Bramble's flowers tasted the best!

At the end, the judge is always given a bunch of flowers as a small, thankyou gift. Aunty was very pleased... She ate it!

Super Snakes

One morning, Seymour Snake's dad, Seymour Senior, said, "I have a surprise, son! Your cousin Sadie is coming to visit!"

"SSSensational!" said Seymour. "We'll have so much fun playing together, just like we did when we were little!"

"Sadie may have changed a bit since you last saw her," said Seymour Senior. "She's been going to Madame Sylvia's Snake School."

Later that day, Seymour slithered down the path to greet his cousin. "Sadie!" cried Seymour. "It's so good to see you! Come and meet my friends!" Seymour said eagerly. "You can play games with us, and…"

"Oh, I can't play games," Sadie interrupted. "Madame Sylvia always says, 'A well-behaved snake may slither and glide and wriggle and slide, but we DON'T swing or sway, or climb or play!'"

"You don't climb trees and swing from branches?" asked Seymour.

"Certainly not!" said Sadie.

"Well, will you come and meet my friends?" Seymour asked hopefully.

"Oh course," said Sadie. "It would be rude not to!"

"HEY, SEYMOUR!" shouted Maxine Monkey. "Come and play with us!"

"Sure!" said Seymour. "By the way, this is my cousin Sadie."

"HI, SADIE!" shouted Mickey. Maxine and Mickey always shouted! "You can come and play, too."

"No, thank you," said Sadie. "I'll just watch. I don't swing or sway, or climb or play." Sadie watched as Seymour climbed a tree, hooked his tail round a branch, and hung down with his mouth open.
Mickey and Maxine threw coconuts for him to catch.

"It really is fun, Sadie," Seymour called to his cousin. "Are you sure you don't want to try?"

"It looks good," Sadie admitted, "but no. Thank you anyway."

The game had just finished when Penelope Parrot arrived. After Seymour had introduced her to Sadie, Penelope asked if they would help her practise her stunt flying.

"Sure, Penelope!" said Seymour and wound himself round the branch to make two loops. With a whooosh Penelope zoomed through the loops.

Seymour spent hours hanging and swinging and climbing – he even climbed to the very top of a tree to talk to Jeremy Giraffe. Each time, Seymour invited Sadie to join him. And each time, Sadie looked more tempted – but she always said the same thing: "I mustn't swing or sway, or climb or play."

Later, Seymour spoke to his dad. "I'm sure Sadie wants to play with me and my friends," he said. "But she insists on only watching. How can I get her to join in?"

"The only way," said Seymour Senior, "is to get Sadie to see for herself how much fun she could be having."

Suddenly, Seymour had an idea.

"Thanks, Dad," he said. "That's just what I'll do!"

The next morning, Sadie was showing Seymour how gracefully she could glide, when suddenly there was a cry of "OH, NO!" Ellen, Emma and Eric Elephant were staring up into a tree. They looked very upset.

"What's wrong?" Sadie asked.

"We were playing Fling the Melon," said Ellen, "and it got stuck in the tree. Our trunks aren't long enough to reach it!"

"Oh, dear," said Sadie. "I'm sure Seymour will be happy to climb up and get it back for you. Won't you, Seymour? Seymour, where are you?"

Seymour had disappeared!

"Can't you help us, Sadie?" asked Emma.

"I'm sorry," said Sadie, "but I DON'T swing or sway…"

"…or climb or play," Emma finished. "We know about Madame Sylvia's rules. But didn't she also teach you that it's important to help others?" she asked.

"Well," said Sadie, "she did say that we must never pass up a chance to do a good deed."

"And this would be a good deed!" said Eric. "We would be so grateful!"

"I'll do it!" Sadie decided.

Up Sadie went, winding round the trunk, weaving her way up into the branches, until she reached the melon at the very top.

"Here it comes!" she shouted to the elephants, giving the melon a shove with her nose. It fell straight down into Ellen's waiting trunk. Then, with a quick wriggle, Sadie coiled herself round the branch and hung upside down above the elephants.

"This is SSSTUPENDOUS!" Sadie shouted. "I haven't had so much fun in years!"

She swung herself over to another tree, "WHEEEEEE!" she cried.

"I knew you'd enjoy this," said Seymour, slithering out from his hiding place. "You just had to try!"

"Come up, Seymour!" Sadie called. "We can swing and sway together."

"Here I come, Sadie," said Seymour, whizzing up the tree. "But what will you tell Madame Sylvia when you go back to school?"

"I'll tell her," said Sadie, "that we MUST climb and play, and swing and sway – ALL DAY!"

To which Seymour and his friends could only add a loud, "Hip-hip-HOORAY!"

Bottoms Up!

The time had come for Doris the duck to teach her ducklings to dive. "It's easy, little ducklings," she quacked. "You bob your heads under the water and put your bottoms in the air. Just remember that — heads down, bottoms up!"

The ducklings nodded excitedly and had a go. Quite a few managed it first time.

"Oooh!" squeaked one. "There are lots of interesting things down there!"

"Exactly!" cried Doris. "And that is why you must all learn to dive. Only we ducks know what goes on under the water."

All afternoon, the ducklings practised. Heads down! Bottoms up! One by one, they got the hang of it.

"Oh, Mummy, look! There are tiny fishes flashing about under here!" squealed one.

"And there's an old bucket, too!" called out another.

"I've found a squiggly thing," quacked a third, "and it tastes lovely!"

By teatime, all the ducklings could dive except for one.

"What's the matter, Dylan?" asked Doris.

"I'm afraid I might not come up again," whispered the little duckling.

"But, Dylan," quacked Doris, "to pop right up again, all you have to do is put your head up and your bottom down!"

Even so, Dylan still didn't want to try. Doris was as encouraging as she could be, but, when the sun began to set, even she was becoming a little bit impatient.

"All ducks dive, Dylan," she said. "You just have to do it. Go on! One, two, three, DIVE!"

But still Dylan hesitated. "I'm going to be one of those ducks who doesn't dive," he said. "I can't see the point. I'm not sure I want to stick my head under the water, it's cold down there. And I might not be able to put my head up again when my tail is up in the air. And I don't want to catch lots of squiggly wiggly things, even if they do taste nice, they might tickle my beak!"

Doris didn't say a word.
Then she had an idea…

"Supper time!" called
Doris. All the little
ducklings bobbed their
heads up.

"We're not hungry!" they
called. "We've been eating
fishes and squiggly things
and delicious duckweed all day."

"I haven't," said Dylan. "I'm really hungry."

So Doris dived down and found him a nice fish.

"Here you are, Dylan," she quacked as she bobbed up. "Oops!"

As Doris spoke, the fish dropped from her beak and disappeared into
the water.

"My supper!" cried Dylan. Down went his head! Up went his bottom!
And he dived quickly down and caught his dinner.

"I did it!" he cried, bobbing up again.

"Well done!" laughed Doris, happily. "But please don't talk with your mouth full, dear!"

Big Top

I t was a grey day in the higgledy-piggledy, messy alley. Harvey and his gang were fed up!

"I'm bored!" moaned Ruffles. "There's nothing to do!"

"What about a game of hide-and-seek?" asked Harvey.

"Boring! Boring!" called Puddles, hanging upside down on the fence.

"What we need is some fun!" yawned Bonnie. "I've got an idea... "

Soon Bonnie and Puddles were jumping on an old mattress. BOINGG! BOINGG! BOINGG! They bounced up and down, up and down.

"*This* is fun!" shrieked Puddles. "I bet I can bounce the highest."

"I'm the Amazing Bouncing Bonnie," giggled Bonnie. "Look!"

She bounced high into the air—and landed with a thud on a clump of grass! "Ooops-a-daisy," she said. "I think I missed!"

Then Mac clambered onto the clothesline.

"WHEEEE! Look at me! I'm the wibbly wobbly dog."

"Oh no!" gasped Patchy. "Here comes tumble-time,"

as Mac toppled over onto the mattress below. Mac sat up and rubbed his head, grinning.

Harvey laughed. His friends' tricks had given him an idea. "Let's put on a circus," he said.

The Alley Dogs all agreed and they scampered off to the playground in search of their big top!

"Okay, everyone," said Harvey, when they arrived. "First, we need to make a circus ring."

"Do you think these old tyres will make good seats?" asked Ruffles.

"They sure will," said Patchy. "And these old plastic bags can be the curtains!"

In no time at all, the big top was ready.

"Well done! We must let everyone know that the circus is in town!" said Harvey. "Come on, Ruffles, you've got the loudest voice."

So, Ruffles took a deep breath and boomed out loud, "Roll up! Roll up! Come to Harvey's Big Top. See the Greatest Show on Earth!"

Soon the air was filled with woofing and yapping as their pals queued up to see the circus!

The nervous gang huddled behind the curtain.

"Right," said Harvey. "Who's going first?"

Patchy peeped out. "Not me!" she whispered. "There are far too many dogs out there and I'm a bit shy."

"And I'm still practising!" cried Ruffles.

The others shook their heads; no one wanted to go first. They were all scaredy-cats!

Harvey crept behind the curtain. His friends were quivering and quaking. "Silly billies," he smiled. "There's nothing to be scared of. Watch me."

He quickly pulled on a cape and ran back into the ring.

"Let the show begin with Harvey the Brave!" he cried, and the audience gave a loud cheer.

"For my first trick," he announced, "the Tricky Tightrope!" He wibbled and wobbled across the top of the swing from one end to the other – and didn't fall off once.

"How does he do it?" gasped the audience, holding their breath in wonder. "Whatever next?"

Harvey climbed to the top of a huge pile of bricks.

"Eeek! What if he falls?" squeaked a little dog. "I can't bear to look."

But Harvey made it – *and* balanced on one paw!

The Alley Dogs peeped out from behind the curtain. Harvey was having such a good time that it didn't look in the least bit scary. So at last, Harvey's Amazing Daring Dogs rushed to join in the fun.

"Look at me," said Ruffles. "I can balance a ball on my tummy."

The audience laughed and cheered and clapped.

Patchy and Mac tumbled and turned on their bouncy mattress – what a pair of acrobats!

The show ended with the dangerous and daring Trolley Trick. Everyone held their breath. Bonnie and Ruffles stood on the bottom, Patchy and Mac climbed onto their shoulders and little Puddles balanced on the very tip-top. When they were ready, Harvey pushed the trolley round and round the ring.

"More! More!" roared the crowd, as the show came to an end.

"Well, Puddles," smiled Harvey, when they finally got back to their higgledy-piggledy, messy alley, "was that boring, boring, boring?"

"Oh no, Harvey," she said. "It wasn't boring, it was fun, fun, fun!"

Custard's New Home

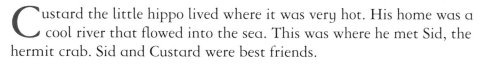

Custard the little hippo lived where it was very hot. His home was a cool river that flowed into the sea. This was where he met Sid, the hermit crab. Sid and Custard were best friends.

This was a bit odd because they were as different as could be. Custard was a lot bigger than Sid for a start. Custard thought that being a hermit crab must be really cool. Instead of having one shell like ordinary crabs, they keep changing from one shell to another.

At the moment Sid had a bright pink, pointed shell. He carried it around with him everywhere he went. Custard thought this was really great. He wanted to carry his own home around with him! Then he wouldn't have to stay out in the hot sun. Hippos don't like getting hot. But there are no shells as big as a hippo. So they have to stay in the river to keep cool.

"Will you help me build my own home?" Custard asked Sid one day.

"Of course I will," said Sid. So they built a house of leaves and tied it to Custard's back. Custard was as pleased as could be. They went for a walk by the river. Sid wore a new round blue shell this time. He said it was the latest fashion. They passed a lion that had a bad cold. ATISHOO!

The lion sneezed loudly and blew Custard's new house away!

"Bother!" said Custard.

So they built another house, this time of bamboo.

"This won't blow away," said Custard.

But an elephant appeared. And, oh dear! Bamboo is an elephant's favourite food.

"Yummy!" said the elephant. "Thanks for bringing me my breakfast!" And he stuffed Custard's house into his mouth!

"That was my new home," said Custard crossly.

"Oops! Sorry," said the elephant.

Sid was looking for a new home for himself. The blue one was getting too small. He thought a yellow one would be nice. A large bird flying lazily overhead spotted Sid without his shell.

"Ah, crab lunch!" it said, and, swooping low, it grabbed Sid in its claws. Sid wriggled and freed himself. He dropped to the ground with a thump.

Custard rushed to help, but was too big and slow. Looking round, he spotted a deckchair, a sunshade and a bucket and spade.

"Quick," he called to Sid, "over here!" Sid dived under the bucket. Just in time! The bird squawked angrily, and flew away. Custard wriggled his bottom into the stripy deck chair, and settled down under the shade of the green umbrella. It felt nice and cool.

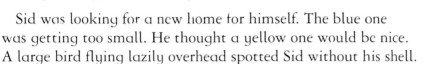

If only his head and legs didn't stick out in front. He wriggled a bit more trying to get comfortable.

"Sid, I've been thinking. I'll just keep cool in the river like I did before," said Custard.

"And I think I'll look for another shell," said Sid.

The two friends wandered back down to the river, happy to be going home together.

131

The Ugly Duckling

Once upon a time, there was a mother duck who laid a clutch of six beautiful little eggs. One day, she looked into her nest in amazement. For there were her six small eggs but lying next to them was another egg that was much, much bigger than the others. "That's odd," she thought, and went back to sitting on the nest.

Soon, one by one, the smaller eggs hatched, and out came six pretty yellow ducklings. Yet the bigger egg still had not hatched.

The mother duck sat on the large egg for another day and another night until eventually the egg cracked, and out tumbled a seventh duckling.

But this one was very different. He was big, with scruffy grey feathers and large brown feet.

"You do look different from my other chicks," exclaimed the mother duck, "but never mind. I'm sure you've got a heart of gold." And she cuddled him to her with all the other ducklings. Sure enough, he was very sweet-natured and happily played alongside the other ducklings.

One day, the mother
duck led her ducklings
down to the river to
learn to swim. One by
one they jumped into
the water and splashed
about. But when the big
grey duckling leaped
into the water he swam

beautifully. He could swim faster and further than any of his brothers
or sisters. The other ducklings were jealous and began to resent him.

"You're a big ugly duckling," they hissed at him. "You don't belong
here." And when their mother wasn't looking they chased him right
away.

The ugly duckling felt very sad as he waddled away across the fields.
"I know I'm not fluffy and golden like my brothers and sisters," he said
to himself. "I may have scruffy grey feathers and big brown feet, but
I'm just as good as they are – and I'm better at swimming!" He sat
down under a bush and started to cry. Just then he heard the sound of
a dog. Only a short way from where he was hiding, a dog rushed past
him, sniffing the ground. The ugly duckling did not dare to move.
He stayed under the bush until it was dark and only then did he feel it
was safe to come out.

He set off, not knowing which way he was going until eventually,
through the darkness, he saw a light shining.
The light came from a cosy-looking cottage.
The ugly duckling looked inside cautiously.
He could see a fire burning in the hearth and
sitting by the fire was an old woman with a
hen and a cat.

"Come in, little duckling," said the old woman. "You are welcome to stay here."

The ugly duckling was glad to warm himself by the fire. When the old lady had gone to bed, the hen and the cat cornered the duckling.

"Can you lay eggs?" enquired the hen.

"No," replied the duckling.

"Can you catch mice?" demanded the cat.

"No," replied the miserable duckling.

"Well, you're no use then, are you?" they sneered.

The next day, the old woman scolded the duckling: "You've been here a whole day and not one egg! You're no use, are you?"

So the ugly duckling waddled off out of the cottage. "I know when I'm not wanted," he said to himself mournfully.

He wandered along for a very long time until at last he reached a lake where he could live without anyone to bother him. He lived on the lake for many months. Gradually the days got shorter and the nights longer. The wind blew the leaves off the trees. Winter came and the weather turned bitterly cold. The lake froze over and the ugly duckling shivered under the reeds at the lake's edge. He was desperately cold, hungry and lonely, but he had nowhere else to go.

At last spring came, the weather got warmer and the ice on the lake melted. The ugly duckling felt the sun on his feathers. "I think I'll go for a swim," he thought. He swam right out into the middle of the lake, where the water was as clear as a mirror. He looked down at his reflection in the water and stared and stared. Staring back at him was a beautiful white bird with a long, elegant neck. "I'm no longer an ugly duckling," he said to himself, "but what am I?"

At that moment three big white birds just like himself flew towards him and landed on the lake. They swam right up to him and one of them said, "You are the handsomest swan that we have ever seen. Would you care to join us?"

"So that's what I am – I'm a swan," thought the bird that had been an ugly duckling. "I would love to join you," he said to the other swans. "Am I really a swan?" he asked, not quite believing it could be true.

"Of course you are!" replied the others. "You're just like us!"

The three older swans became his best friends and the ugly duckling, that was now a beautiful swan, swam across the lake with them and there they lived together. He knew that he was one of them and that he would never be lonely again.

Bouncy Bunny

Mummy Rabbit had four beautiful babies. Three of them were tiny, soft balls of fluff – they were cuddly, quiet and very, very cute. They never made a noise and always did exactly what their mummy told them.

And then there was Benny!

Benny wasn't like his brother and sisters at all. He was large and loud and he had the biggest bunny feet in the whole world. And he loved to bounce! From dawn to dusk, Benny bounced everywhere – THUMP! THUMP! THUMP! Benny never did what Mummy Rabbit told him, but she loved him just the same.

Early one morning, Mummy Rabbit was woken by a very loud noise that made the whole burrow wibble and wobble. Soon, everyone was wide awake. What was that noise?

It was Benny, of course, bouncing and boinging around the burrow on his big, flat feet! "I'm *sure* he doesn't mean to be so noisy," said Mummy Rabbit, with a big yawn.

Benny bounced outside. Mummy Rabbit followed him, twitching her nose and checking for danger – *where had he disappeared to?*

Suddenly, there was a loud THUMP! THUMP! THUMP!

"I'm hungry," said Benny, bouncing past her. "I want my breakfast now, Mummy!" By the time all the bunnies had come out of the burrow and into the sunshine, Benny had bounced round the meadow three times!

"Benny, stop jumping around!" said Mummy Rabbit. "Stay with the others. It's dangerous out here."

"Now then, children," whispered Mummy Rabbit. "We're going over to the carrot field for breakfast. You must all stay very close to me and don't wander from the path."

But, of course, Benny didn't listen. With one huge bounce he disappeared through a hole in the hedge and was gone!

"Oh, dear! Oh, dear! Oh, dear!" said his mother. "What is he up to now?"

"Benny Bunny!" said Mummy Rabbit. "Where did you get that lettuce?"

"In that field!" replied Benny.

"You might have been caught," said Mummy.

"I'm much too fast!" said Benny.

"Hurry, children," said Mummy Rabbit. "We must get to the carrot field before the farmer starts work."

But, of course, Benny wasn't listening. He was nibbling a dandelion. "Hmm, tasty!" he mumbled to himself.

"Benny Bunny!" called Mummy Rabbit, crossly. "Stop that munching and follow me!" Mummy Rabbit hopped under the gate and into the field. She collected lots of crunchy carrots. "Remember," she warned her bunnies. "Eat as much as you can, but stay close to me and watch out for the farmer."

The carrots were wonderful – fat and juicy and crisp. Soon, Benny's brother and sisters were all chewing happily. Benny bounced around on his big, flat feet, nibbling and munching as he went. Boing! Boing! Boing!

Mummy Rabbit and her bunnies munched their way across the field, nibbling a leaf here, crunching a carrot there. No one noticed that little Tufty, Benny's baby brother, wasn't following them.

Suddenly, Mummy Rabbit heard the roar of the tractor. "Quick!" she cried. "The farmer's coming!" Everyone hopped into the hedge – except Tufty!

BOUNCY BUNNY

Mummy Rabbit saw the tractor heading straight for Tufty. Its big wheels were squashing everything in its path. Her little baby crouched by the fence, his paws over his eyes, too terrified to move.

What could Mummy Rabbit do? Suddenly, Benny Bunny bounced past! In one huge bound, Benny was by Tufty's side. He bounced his brother out of the way, just before the tractor ran over him!

"I told you I was fast," giggled Benny.

"Benny Bunny!" said Mummy Rabbit, hopping over to Tufty and Benny. "You're so… "

"I know! I know!" said Benny. "I'm so *bouncy*!"

"Oh, yes!" said Mummy Rabbit. "I'm so glad that you *are* such a bouncy bunny!" and she gave him a great big kiss.

Fierce Tiger

Tiger wasn't really a tiger. He was a fierce stray kitten. People called him Tiger because he hissed and arched his back whenever they came near. "You really should be nicer to people," said his friend Tibbles. "They're not so bad once you train them."

But Tiger didn't trust people. If they came too near, he would show his claws and even give them a scratch. That soon taught them not to mess with Tiger. Tiger looked after himself. He didn't need anyone. At night he wandered the streets, searching dustbins for scraps and stealing food put out for pets. During the day, he slept wherever he could – under a bush, on top of a garage, and sometimes under the cars in an old scrap yard.

One cold winter's night, Tiger was wandering the streets when it began to snow. He spotted an open window.

"Aha," thought Tiger. "I bet it's warm and dry in there." He jumped through the window and found himself in a dark porch.

"This will do," thought Tiger. Tiger curled into a ball and was soon fast asleep. He was so comfortable that he slept all through the night. When he finally awoke, there was no one around. But beside him were a bowl of food and a dish of water.

"Don't mind if I do," purred Tiger. He gobbled down the whole lot, then drank some water before leaving through the window again. That day was colder than any Tiger had ever known so, when night fell and he saw the window open once more, he didn't hesitate to sneak in. This time, Tiger could see that the door from the porch was slightly ajar. He pushed it open and found himself in a warm kitchen. So he settled down and had a wonderful night's sleep. When he awoke in the morning, he found a bowl of delicious fish and a dish of water beside him.

"Don't mind if I do," purred Tiger. And he wolfed down the fish and lapped up the water before leaving. That night it was still snowing. Tiger returned once more. This time, when he went to settle himself beside the fire, he found a cosy basket there.

"Don't mind if I do," purred Tiger. And he crawled in and went to sleep. Tiger had never slept so well. In the morning, Tiger was woken by a rattling sound. Someone was in the kitchen. Tiger opened his left eye just a crack. A little boy was placing a bowl beside the basket. Tiger opened his eyes and stared at the little boy. The little boy stared at Tiger. Tiger leapt to his feet and got ready to hiss and scratch.

"Good boy," whispered the little boy, gently.

Tiger looked at the bowl. It was full of milk. "Don't mind if I do," he purred, and he drank the lot.

After that, Tiger returned to the house every night. Before long, he never slept anywhere else. The little boy always gave him plenty to eat and drink. And, in return, Tiger let the little boy stroke him and hold him on his lap.

One morning, Tiger was playing with the little boy in the garden, when his old friend Tibbles strolled past.

"I thought you didn't like people," meowed Tibbles.

"Oh," smiled Tiger, "they seem to be okay once you train them."

Tiger was no longer a fierce stray kitten!

Snap Happy

One lazy morning, Claudia Crocodile was drifting down the river, looking for fun. Up ahead, she could see Mickey and Maxine Monkey and Chico Chimp playing on the riverbank. "I think I'll give them a fright," decided Claudia. "It's always amusing to watch them run away!"

Flashing and gnashing her sharp teeth, she swam towards the three friends. Sure enough, the SNAP! SNAP! SNAP! of Claudia's jaws scared the little monkeys.

"RUN," cried Maxine, "before she snaps our tails off!"

They tumbled over each other as they climbed to safety.

"Hee, hee!" Claudia laughed as she watched them. "Scaring the monkeys is such fun!"

That afternoon, Claudia was bored again, so she looked for someone else to frighten. "Aha!" she said. "There's little Timmy Tiger, paddling all by himself. I'll give him a real fright!" And she set off down the river, SNAP-SNAP-SNAPPING as she went.

Timmy didn't hear Claudia, until she was right behind him! SNAP! SNAP! went her great big jaws. GNASH! GNASH! GNASH! went her sharp, pointy teeth.

"AAAAGGGGGHHH!" screamed Timmy, as he saw Claudia's mouth open wide. He tried to run away, but his paws were stuck in the mud!

Claudia came closer and closer. Timmy trembled with terror.

"You're supposed to run away!" Claudia whispered.

"I c-c-can't," stammered Timmy. "I'm stuck!"

"Oh," said Claudia, disappointed. "It's no fun if you don't run away."

"Aren't you g-going to eat me?" gulped Timmy.

"EAT YOU?" roared Claudia. "Yuck! You're all furry! I prefer fish."

"Really?" said Timmy. "Then why are you always snapping and gnashing and frightening everyone?"

"Because that's what crocodiles do!" said Claudia. "We're supposed to be scary. Er... you won't tell anyone I didn't eat you, will you?" she asked, helping Timmy climb out of the mud.

"Don't worry," laughed Timmy, "I won't tell!"

"Thanks for un-sticking me," Timmy said. "I never knew you could be nice. I like you!"

Claudia's green face blushed bright red!

"I think everyone would like you," went on Timmy, "if you just tried to be friendly, instead of scary."

"Oh, I don't think I can do that," said Claudia. "My jaws simply HAVE to snap and my teeth just MUST gnash! I can't help it."

"Wait!" said Timmy. "I know just how you can be friendly and helpful and snap and gnash at the same time! Here's your chance."

As Timmy and Claudia went along together, they saw Mickey and Maxine trying to smash open some coconuts.

Claudia swam towards the monkeys, SNAP-SNAP-SNAPPING with her jaws. As soon as they heard her, the monkeys ran for the nearest tree.

"I just want to help," said Claudia, climbing on to the bank. "Throw me a coconut!" And with a SNAP! SNAP! SNAP! quick as a flash, Mickey's coconut was open. Then Claudia opened Maxine's coconut, too and soon everyone was sharing the cool, refreshing milk and chewy chunks of coconut. Claudia had never shared anything and found that she liked it!

Chico Chimp came running towards his friends. He was carrying a big watermelon. Suddenly, Chico spotted Claudia, whose jaw was open, ready to SNAP! "Uh-oh!" he gulped, turning to run.

"Don't worry, Chico," said Maxine. "Throw Claudia the watermelon!"

Chico watched in amazement as Claudia SNAP-SNAP-SNAPPED the watermelon into neat slices for everyone. "Thanks, Claudia!" they all chorused. Chico gave Claudia the biggest slice.

Then Emma, Eric and Ellen Elephant came trundling down to the river with bundles of thick branches in their trunks. "We're going to make a raft!" said Emma — and then they saw Claudia.

As the frightened elephants galloped away, Claudia picked up the branches they had dropped. SNAP! SNAP! GNASH! GNASH! went Claudia's strong jaws and sharp teeth.

"Wow! Thanks, Claudia!" said Emma, as the elephants came back. "That was really helpful!"

Claudia grinned. Being friendly and helpful was rather nice!

"Here we go!" shouted the elephants, when their raft was ready. The friends on the riverbank watched them.

"That looks like so much fun!" said Chico. "Can you help us make a raft, too, Claudia?"

"I can do even better," said Claudia. "Hop on my back!"

"WHEEE! This is GREAT!" whooped Maxine as they sailed down the river on Claudia's back.

Happiest of all was Claudia, who had found that having friends was much more fun than scaring them!

Lost for Ever

Sheep are lovely animals, but they are not the cleverest creatures. They follow one another without thinking too much about whether it is a good idea. When the leader is Maria, it very often isn't!

One day, Maria thought that the grass in the next meadow was much greener and juicier than the grass right under her nose.

"Come on, girls!" she baa-ed. "Follow me!"

With a skip and a jump, Maria was over the fence and into the meadow next door, and it wasn't long before the other sheep had followed Maria into the next field, too.

After an hour of munching grass in the new meadow, Maria happened to look over the wall on the far side. The grass there looked even better. "Follow me!" she baa-ed again, and she was off! The other sheep were right behind her.

By the end of the afternoon, Maria and her friends found themselves a very long way from Old MacDonald's farm and seemed likely to be lost for ever!

"I don't know where we are," said Maria, looking all around her. "Oh, I can't think now. I'm going to sleep."

And, of course, all the other sheep were soon asleep, too.

Now, when sheep wake up, they are hungry! So the next morning, when Maria awoke, she forgot about trying to find her way home. Instead, she tucked into some tasty grass.

You can guess what the other sheep did!

Maria grazed her way across the meadow and came to a hedge. Over the hedge was another meadow, and the grass looked even tastier there. "Follow me, girls!" Maria baa-ed. So, with a skip, a jump and a leap, the flock bounded into the meadow and started on their mid-morning snack.

At lunch time, tea time and supper time, exactly the same thing happened.

It wasn't until it was bedtime that Maria remembered that they were a long way from home. "We must be even further now," she baa-ed, sadly.

"But maaamaaa…" bleated her little lamb.

"Tell me in the morning," Maria replied.

"But maaamaaa…" the lamb tried again.

"Go to sleep, little one," said Maria. "We'll get home tomorrow."

"But MAAAMAAA!" laughed the little lamb. "We are home already. Look! What can you see?"

And, sure enough, there before them was Old MacDonald's meadow.

The smoke from the farmhouse chimney drifted into the evening air. Old MacDonald stood by the gate. Without intending to, Maria had led them all the way back home again.

Although sheep are not clever creatures, sometimes they are silly in a very clever way – if you see what I mean!

Fire! Fire!

The sun was shining in the higgledy-piggledy, messy alley.
"It's much too hot!" Hattie thought to herself, as she tried to find
a nice shady spot for a snooze. Her kittens, Lenny and Lulu, were cat-
napping under the apple tree and she knew from the loud snoring that
Uncle Bertie and Auntie Lucy were fast asleep in their dustbins.
Everyone was hiding from the sun – everyone except Cousin Archie!

Archie was lying on top of the fence, slurping his third bottle of milk!
He didn't notice the sun's rays shining through the glass of those empty
milk bottles. It was focused right onto Hattie's dustbin full of old
newspapers – the perfect place for a fire to start!

Suddenly, Hattie's nose twitched. "What's that?" she wondered.
"It smells like smoke."

"It is smoke!" she gasped, as she saw
bright red and yellow flames leaping out
of her dustbin.

"F-Fire!" she cried. "Help!"

"Wake up, Bertie!" cried Hattie.
"My dustbin's on fire!"

Uncle Bertie's sleepy head popped
up from his dustbin.

"I must have been dreaming, Hattie!"

he yawned. "I dreamt that your bin was on fire."

"It wasn't a dream," cried Hattie. "My bin *is* on fire."

Cousin Archie fell off the fence in shock! He landed right on top of poor Bertie!

"Hurry!" urged Hattie. "We must put the fire out."

All the shouting woke the twins from their dreams.

"Mummy! Mummy!" they meowed, "what's happening?"

Hattie grabbed her kittens and put them on the top of the fence, well away from the dangerous fire.

"You'll be safe here," she told them.

Uncle Bertie knew he had to find some water quickly.

"Over there!" Hattie said, pointing to an old bucket by the fence.

"Hooray!" cried Bertie, finding the bucket half full of water. "It might just be enough to put out the fire."

"Cousin Archie!" he cried. "Come and help me."

The two cats ran down the alley, carrying the bucket between them.

Then, with smoke billowing all around, Archie and Bertie aimed the bucket of water and let go...

SPLOSH! There was a huge sizzling sound.

"Hooray!" Bertie cried, with a sigh of relief. "We've done it!"

But suddenly, a spark from the fire landed on the rubbish next to the dustbin.

"Oh no, we haven't!" wailed Archie. "Now the rubbish is on fire!"

"Quick," Hattie said to Archie. "We need more help. Go and wake up the dogs."

At the other end of the alley, the dogs were all fast asleep.

"Help!" shrieked Archie, as he hurtled towards them. "Hattie's bin is on fire. It's spreading down the alley and we can't put it out."

But no one stirred. Archie was always playing tricks on the Alley Dogs and today it was just too hot to bother. Harvey opened one eye lazily.

"That's a good one, Archie," he said. "But you'll have to try harder than that."

"It's true!" Archie shouted, desperately. "Look!"

Harvey sat up slowly. "This had better not be one of your tricks, Archie," he growled. Then he shaded his eyes from the sun and looked up the alley. As soon as he saw the billowing smoke, he knew the Alley Cat was telling the truth.

"Archie's right!" barked Harvey. "Quick, everyone to the rescue!"

The dogs raced up the alley towards the fire. Even little Puddles wanted to help. But Harvey scooped her up and placed her on the fence by the kittens.

"You can't do a thing, Puddles!" he said. "Just stay here."

The alley was filled with smelly black smoke. All the cats were coughing and choking. But Harvey knew just what to do.

"Quick!" he said. "Everybody to the water-barrel. Use anything you can to gather the water."

Grabbing old buckets and cans, the cats and dogs formed a long line. Auntie Lucy stood by the barrel to fill up the containers. Then, splishing and splashing, they passed the water along the line to Harvey, who threw it over the fire.

Suddenly, Lucy gave a cry. "The water's run out!"

"Oh no!" said Archie. "We'll never put the fire out now."

The Alley Cats and Dogs stared in dismay. What could they do? They must have more water.

"Oh, no! We're going to lose our lovely home," wailed Hattie, bursting into tears.

Suddenly, Lenny had an idea. "I know what to do," he coughed. Grabbing his sister and Puddles, he pulled them over the fence.

"I've just remembered what's in this garden," said Lenny, disappearing into the long grass.

When he came back, he was pulling a hose.

"Mummy!" cried Lenny. "Look what we've got."

Fire! Fire!

Hattie peered through the smoke and gasped. Harvey grabbed the nozzle, as Bertie leapt over the fence and raced to turn on the tap.

With a mighty spurt, the water sploshed out, drenching the blazing boxes and soaking the smouldering bins. Everyone cheered! Some of the water splashed over the cats and dogs – but they didn't care. The fizzling, sizzling fire was out!

"You little ones deserve a treat for saving our alley!" barked Harvey. "Puppy snacks for you, Puddles, and kitty nibbles for the twins."

"Three cheers for Lenny, Lulu and Puddles!" cried Archie.

"Hip-hip-hooray!"

Hippo's Holiday

It was a warm, sunny morning in the jungle.

"A perfect time for a long, relaxing wallow," thought Howard Hippo. Wallowing in the river was Howard's favourite thing to do. He found a nice, cool, muddy spot and settled in. Howard was just drifting off into a delightful daydream, when… SPLASH! "Gotcha!" shrieked Maxine Monkey. SPLOOSH! "Gotcha back!" shouted Chico Chimp.

"Can't you monkeys and chimps play somewhere else?" Howard grumbled. "I'm wallowing here!"

"Oops! Sorry, Howard," Maxine apologised. But it was too late. Howard's wallow was ruined. That afternoon, as the hot sun beat down on his back, Howard slithered into the river to cool off.

"Aaah," he breathed, as he soaked in the cool water. "This is sooo lovely."

"Yoo-hoo! Howard!" called Penelope Parrot. "I've just learned to do a double-rollover-loop-the-loop! Want to see?"

"Sure, Penelope," sighed Howard. It didn't look as if he was going to have a chance to relax this afternoon, either! The next morning, Howard's cousin, Hilary, came to visit.

"You look exhausted, Howard," she said.

"That's because I never have a chance to relax and wallow any more," said Howard.

"What you need is a holiday," said Hilary. "I'm leaving for Hippo

Hollow this afternoon. Why don't you come with me?"

"That sounds like a good idea!" said Howard.

"You'll love Hippo Hollow," said Hilary, as the two hippos trundled through the jungle. "There's so much mud!"

Howard saw himself relaxing in a cool mud bath.

"And there are streams and waterfalls!"continued Hilary. Howard imagined having lots of cool showers.

"And everyone has lots and lots of FUN!" finished Hilary.

Howard thought about playing games with new hippo friends.

At last Howard and Hilary arrived at Hippo Hollow. "It's even more beautiful than I had imagined!" Howard exclaimed.

"And it looks like we've arrived just in time!" said Hilary.

"For what?" asked Howard. "A relaxing mud bath?" "No, silly!" laughed Hilary. "Hippo-robics!"

"Let's get moving, everyone!" called a sleek-looking hippo. Lots of other hippos galloped into the stream behind her.

"Come on, Howard," said Hilary. "Don't be a party pooper on the first day of your holiday!"

Howard had no choice but to join in. "Kick, two, three, four! Kick, two, three, four!" shouted the instructor.

Howard did his best and kicked with all the others. "Surely everyone will want a nice, long rest after all this exercise?" he thought. But he was wrong! After a quick shower in the waterfall, everyone rushed off to play Volley-Melon and Hilary wanted Howard on her team. Howard finally did get to have a rest after lunch – but not for long! "You're looking much more relaxed, Howard," Hilary called, as she led her junior swimming class right past him. "This holiday was just what you needed, wasn't it?"

"Er… I guess so," Howard replied, weakly. After his busy day, Howard was hoping for an early night. He was just getting settled, when he heard Hilary.

"Come on, Howard!" she bellowed. "You don't want to miss the Hippo-Hooray Cabaret! They are really good!"

"Oh – YAWN – how wonderful," sighed Howard. He could barely keep his eyes open.

The next morning, Howard was sliding into the river, when he heard Hilary calling.

"Is it time for Hippo-robics?" he asked.

"Oh, no," said Hilary. "Lots of good, fresh air is what you need. So we're going on a hike!" Howard huffed and puffed all through the exhausting hike. "I hope I can have a nice cool bath when this is over," he thought. Howard got his wish. But, as he was soaking his sore muscles, Hilary came by for a chat.

"The hike was fun, wasn't it?" she said.

"Oh yes," said Howard. "In fact, I enjoyed it so much, that I've decided to go on another one!"

"Really?" said Hilary. "That's great! Where are you hiking to?"

"Home!" said Howard. "I'm going home, where I can have a REAL holiday. And where there are no Hippo-robics, and no Volley-Melon games, no cabarets and no one to stop me wallowing as long as I like!" And so that's exactly what Howard did!

The Missing Scarf

Kanga was very proud of her stripy knitted scarf. She had made it herself and she had also made a smaller matching one for her son, Joey. Kanga used to hop through the bush with her scarf streaming out behind her, while Joey's could just be seen poking out of the top of her pouch. Now Joey was older, he was too big for Kanga's pouch, but he still wore his scarf as he hopped along beside his mother.

Then one day Kanga woke up to find that her beautiful scarf was missing. She searched high and low but it was nowhere to be found. Eventually she decided that she would have to go out into the bush to look for it.

"Stay here," she said to Joey. "I'll try not to be long. I'm sure to find my scarf soon." Kanga hopped off into the bush and started to search among the roots of trees and under stones.

She had gone quite a long way when, looking up into the branches of a eucalyptus tree, she spotted Koala. Now Koala was usually asleep, but this time she was preparing a meal of eucalyptus leaves for her children. Kanga looked up at Koala and then her jaw dropped. For Koala was quite clearly wearing Kanga's scarf around her tummy. Then, to Kanga's horror, she saw Koala use the end of the scarf to wipe the teacups! "Koala," Kanga called. "Whatever do you think you're doing?"

Koala stopped cleaning the teacups and looked down through the branches of the eucalyptus tree at Kanga. "I'm wiping my teacups with my apron," she replied sleepily, "and I'll thank you not to interfere!" And with that, she yawned and moved several branches further up the tree.

Poor Kanga felt very embarrassed. How could she have mistaken Koala's striped apron for her own scarf? She hopped away and carried on further into the bush. After a while she heard Kookaburra's familiar laughing call nearby. "I know," thought Kanga, "I'll ask her. She'd be able to spot my scarf easily from the sky." She followed the sound of Kookaburra's call until she came to the tree where she lived. Kanga was about to call up when her jaw dropped again. For Kookaburra was quite clearly carrying Kanga's scarf in her beak. "Kookaburra," Kanga called. "Whatever do you think you're doing?"

"I'm lining my nest," mumbled Kookaburra through a beakful of stripy feathers. "And please don't interfere," she added as she arranged the feathers carefully in place.

Poor Kanga felt even more embarrassed. She carried on further into the bush. After a while she reached a wide, open plain and there she saw Emu running past with his baby chicks on his back. As he rushed past, Kanga's jaw dropped yet again. Emu quite clearly had Kanga's scarf tucked in amongst his chicks.

"Emu, whatever do you think you're doing?" called Kanga.

"I'm taking my chicks to safety," said Emu, glancing up at the sky as he sped away. "And you should do the same," he added. Kanga realised that what she had thought was her scarf were just the striped chicks on Emu's back.

Poor Kanga felt even more embarrassed. Then she felt a few spots of rain on her nose and, looking up, saw a huge black cloud overhead. There was no time to lose – she must find shelter. She made a dash to the edge of the plain and soon found herself by a stream. She wandered along feeling cold, wet, tired and miserable. Finally, she lay down in the wet grass beside the stream and tried to get to sleep. She shivered with cold and wondered how Joey was and whether he was behaving himself. She so hoped he hadn't got into mischief.

Just then there was a tap on her shoulder and there stood Platypus. "I could hear you in my burrow over there," she said pointing towards a hole beside the stream just above the water. "I thought you might like this to keep you warm," she added.

"My scarf!" exclaimed Kanga.

"Oh, *that's* what it is! I'm ever so sorry," said Platypus. "I've been using it as a blanket for my babies.

It's cold and damp in my burrow, you know," she added, rather forlornly. "It was stuck on some thorns and I know I shouldn't have taken it, but I just thought it would be so nice for keeping my young ones warm," blurted Platypus, and she started to sob.

"There now," said Kanga, "don't cry. You can keep the scarf. You need it more than me."

Platypus stopped crying and looked overjoyed. "Thank you," she said.

"No, thank you," said Kanga. "I've learned a lesson, which is not to get upset over a scarf, for I've ended up falling out with my friends."

Kanga made her way back home, but it took a long time because she apologised to all her friends on the way. When she explained what had happened Emu, Kookaburra and Koala all forgave her, and by the time she reached home she was feeling much better. Joey was there to greet her. "What have you been up to while I was away?" she asked.

"I made you this," he said. He handed her a scarf. It was a very funny-looking scarf, made out of twigs, grass and feathers, but Kanga loved it very much.

"This is much more special than my old scarf," she said. And she gave Joey an extra big hug.

Clever Boogie

Boogie was a very clever pig. Most pigs aren't clever. They can't do sums. They can't tie their own shoelaces. Every single day they are given pig food to eat, and they say, "Oink! Oink! Pig food! My favourite!" They don't remember it's always the same.

But Boogie remembered every horrible meal he'd ever had, and was really fed up with pig food. It tasted like minced rubbish! Boogie lived in his own pen. In the field outside the pigpen lived a sheep, a horse and a cow. There were trees in the field too, but none near Boogie.

One day, acorns started falling from the biggest tree. The tree was a long way from Boogie, but just a few acorns bounced over and into his pen. An apple from another tree rolled until it rolled into Boogie's pen.

Now, usually the only thing inside a pigpen is a pig. Pigs eat everything else! They eat the grass, the roots, worms, stinging nettles, everything! All that is left is a pig in mud! Pigs think anything else in a pen must be food. So Boogie ate the acorns.

Acorns are really horrible to eat, but Boogie thought they were delicious! Then he ate the apple. He had never eaten anything so good in his life! He wanted all the acorns and apples! They were all around him, but he could not reach them. Suddenly, he had an idea.

Next to Boogie's pigpen was an old animal shed that had fallen to bits. Bricks and wood were spread about and wavy metal roof panels lay nearby. Boogie said to the cow, "Will you move that metal roof for me? I'll give you some of my food if you do."

"I have all this grass to eat!" said the cow.

"But that's just plain grass," said Boogie. "This is delicious lumps of pig food!"

"Oh, all right!" said the cow. She pushed the roof under the apple tree.

Boogie gave the cow some of his pig food. She chewed for ages before she realised pig food did not have any actual taste in it. She spat it out.

"Pwah! Tastes like minced rubbish!" she said, and trotted off.

Boogie said to the horse, "Will you move that barrel for me? I'll give you some of my food if you do."

"I have all this grass to eat!" said the horse.

"But yours is green grass," said Boogie. "This is rich brown pig food in lumps!" So the horse moved the barrel where Boogie wanted it and was given the rest of the pig food.

"Yuck!" said the horse, when he tried it. "Do you really eat this rubbish?" And he galloped off too.

Boogie looked at the sheep. The sheep said, "I know – you want me to move something! I'll do it, but please don't give me any pig food!"

The sheep moved the drainpipe to where Boogie wanted it.

When the next apple fell, it rolled down the iron roof into the drainpipe and flew into Boogie's pen! An acorn bounced off the barrel, and soon there were apples and acorns falling everywhere and bouncing into Boogie's pen.

Boogie dashed around, catching apples and acorns before they could even touch the ground!

And he never had to eat pig food again!

Troublesome Sister

In the higgledy-piggledy, messy alley it was tidy-up time! Harvey and the gang had worked hard all morning, scribbling and scrabbling in the heaps of junk trying to clean up their home.

At last, the skip was full of rubbish and they could have a break. All the gang settled down for a snooze, except for Puddles, Harvey's little sister.

"Where's my teddy?" she wondered. "And where's my ish?" Puddles' 'ish' was a blanket she'd had since she was a baby. It was full of holes and rather smelly, but she loved it lots.

She looked round the alley. "Teddy! Ish!" she called. "Where are you?" She didn't see them peeping out from the top of the skip.

Puddles was always getting into lots of mischief and today she scampered off down the alley, sure that she would find her teddy and ish down there somewhere. Spotting a hole in the fence, she peeped through and saw an old box of toys. "Are teddy and ish in there?" she wondered.

She squeezed and squashed herself through the gap and crept up to the toybox.

"Teddy! Ish! Are you in there?" she called. But they weren't. She did find an old toy mouse, hidden away at the back. "Doesn't anyone love you?" she asked. "You're very soft and cuddly – I'll love you! Come on, Mousey," she giggled. "You come home with me." Puddles was feeling much happier.

But Lulu the kitten wasn't. The mouse was her favourite toy and as Puddles trotted off she began to wail.

"Mummy! Mummy! Come quickly!" she cried.

Hattie, Lulu's mum, appeared through a gap in the fence. "What a terrible noise you're making," she purred. "What is the matter?"

Lulu sobbed and sniffed. "Mummy! Puddles has taken my Mousey!" cried the kitten.

"There, there," purred Hattie, trying to stop the sobs. "Don't you worry, Lulu, we'll soon get Mousey back."

But Lulu just screamed even louder.

Puddles didn't hear poor Lulu crying. She was dancing around the garden with her new friend. "We are having fun, aren't we, Mousey!" she laughed as she skipped along. "Now all I need is an ish."

As she skipped through the garden next door, Puddles saw a tatty, old scarf hanging down from the branch of an apple tree.

"Oh look, Mousey!" she cried. "A cuddly ish with no one to love it."

"Well, it's not really an ish," she thought, "but it is very, very soft." She reached up and took one end in her mouth. With a pull and a tug, the scarf floated down. Puddles picked it up and cuddled it. Now she was really happy. She didn't see Lenny, Lulu's brother, fast asleep in the flowerbed nearby.

Lenny woke up with a start and suddenly saw Puddles skipping off along the garden with his favourite scarf – the one he had hung in the tree to use as a swing! He couldn't believe his eyes and began to cry. "Mummy! Mummy!" he wailed, loudly.

Hattie and Lulu squeezed through the hedge.

"That naughty Puddles has stolen my scarf," sobbed Lenny.

Hattie sighed. Oh dear, now both her twins were crying. Something would have to be done about that pup!

Just then, Puddles popped through the hedge and ran straight into the angry Alley Cats.

"Oh no!" gulped Puddles. "Someone's in trouble, and I think it's *me*!"

Lulu and Lenny were hiding behind Hattie who looked very cross. Puddles was suddenly scared and she began to cry. "H-H-Harvey!" she croaked. "Help me!"

Puddles' wailing woke up Harvey and the gang.

"Is that Puddles I can hear?" said Ruffles. "Yes! Run, Harvey, *run*! Puddles needs your help!"

"Hang on, Puddles," woofed Harvey. "I'm coming!" And off he ran, as fast as he could go…

Harvey burst through the hedge. "Okay, guys!" he gasped. "What's all the fuss about?"

The angry Alley Cats began shouting all at once.

Puddles hid behind her big brother and shivered and shook. Whatever had she done?

There was so much noise that Harvey couldn't hear a word that anyone was saying.

"QUIET!" he barked. And they were – even the kittens!

"Thank you," said Harvey. "Now then, Hattie, tell me, what is all the noise about?"

"That scallywag sister of yours has stolen my twins' favourite toys," grumbled Hattie.

"Did you, Puddles?" asked Harvey, sternly.

"I didn't mean to, Harvey," she cried. "I thought that no one wanted them."

She gave back little Mousey and the tattered and torn scarf. "Sorry, Lulu," she whimpered. "Sorry, Lenny. I only wanted to love them."

"That's okay, Puddles," smiled the twins. "But you see, we love them – lots and lots."

Hattie looked at Puddles and shook her head, she really was an annoying puppy. Harvey gave a huge sigh – panic over!

"Puddles, you're such a scamp," smiled Harvey.

"But I was only looking for my teddy and my ish,"cried Puddles.

"I don't know where they are."

"Oh, is that what this is all about?" said Harvey.

He scooped them from the skip and gave them back to Puddles with a hug and a kiss. "Now, no more trouble today," he said. "Let's all have a dog-nap."

Puddles hugged her teddy and stroked her ish; she was happy again. "Well," said Puddles, looking at Harvey with a naughty grin, "Ish and I will be good, but Teddy might not!"

Leo Makes a Friend

Leo was quite a shy lion. His mum and dad, and brothers and sisters were all much bolder. Sometimes he was sad because he didn't have any friends.

"Mum," he said one day, "why will no one play with me?"

"They think you're frightening because you're a lion," said Mum.

It was a lovely day. Leo felt sure he would make a new friend today. He came to some trees where a group of small monkeys were playing. When the monkeys saw Leo they scampered to the top of the tallest trees.

"Hello," called out Leo. There was no answer. "Hello," he called again. "Won't you come down and play with me?"

There was silence. Then one of the monkeys blew a loud raspberry.

"Go away," he said rudely, "we don't like lions! Your teeth are too big," said the monkey, and giggled noisily.

Leo walked on until he came to a deep pool where a hippopotamus and her baby were bathing. Leo watched them playing in the water.

"Hi!" called out Leo. "Can I come in the water with you? I'd like to play," said Leo.

"So would I!" said Baby Hippo.

"No, you wouldn't," said Mummy Hippo firmly. "You don't play with lions."

Puzzled, Leo walked on. He came to an ostrich with its head buried in the sand. "What are you doing?" asked Leo in surprise.

"Hiding from you!" said the ostrich gruffly.

"But I can still see you!" said Leo.

"But I can't see you!" said the ostrich.

"Come and play with me instead," said Leo.

"Not likely," said the ostrich. "I don't play with lions, they roar!"

Leo walked on. He saw a snake sunbathing on a rock. He touched the snake gently with his paw. "Play with me," he said.

"Ouch!" said the snake. "Your claws are too sharp."

"I shall just have to get used to playing by myself," he thought.

Suddenly, he heard a small voice say, "Hello!"

Leo looked round. He could see a pair of yellow eyes peeping at him from behind a tree. "You won't want to play with me," said Leo grumpily, "I've got a loud roar, and sharp claws, *and* big teeth!"

"So have I," said the voice.

"What are you?" asked Leo, interested now.

"I'm a lion, of course!"

And into the clearing walked another little lion.

"I'm a lion, too," said Leo, grinning. "Would you like to share my picnic?"

"Yes, please!" said the other lion. They ate the picnic and played for the rest of the afternoon.

"I like being a lion," said Leo happily. He had made a friend at last!

Kissable Kitten

In a corner of the kitchen, Mummy Cat lay in her basket and purred happily. Curled up asleep beside her were four beautiful kittens – a grey kitten called Timmy, a black kitten called Winnie and a stripy kitten called Ginger.

And then there was Kissy, the softest, cutest kitten you ever did see!

Timmy had the biggest blue eyes. They spotted everything. When he and Kissy were in the garden, chasing bumble bees, it was Timmy who spied the water sprinkler.

"Watch out, Kissy!" said Timmy. "You'll get wet!"

"Splish, splash, flipperty-flash!" sang Kissy. "I don't care!" Kissy pushed through the flowers with her little pink nose and shrieked with laughter, as the water sprinkler suddenly covered them both with water.

"Kissy!" spluttered Timmy, shaking water drops from his ears. "Now look what you've done!" But Kissy just rolled around, laughing. "Oh, Timmy," she giggled. "That was so funny!"

KISSABLE KITTEN

"Goodness me," said Mummy Cat, as her kittens dripped water on to the kitchen floor. "Timmy Kitten! You shouldn't have let Kissy get so wet! Now I shall have to dry you both!"

Kissy wriggled and giggled, as Mummy Cat's rough, pink tongue made her wet fur soft and white again. "Sugar and spice, that feels nice!" she sang.

But Timmy wasn't quite so happy. "Ow! Miaow!" he howled, as Mummy Cat's tongue licked him dry.

Kissy loved to explore with Winnie. Winnie had the cutest kitten nose ever and could sniff out all the best yummy food. "Mmm! Smells like jam and cream," said Winnie, her nose and whiskers twitching. Kissy reached up and gently pulled a corner of the tablecloth.

"Mind, Kissy!" said Winnie. "You'll pull everything over!"

"Yum, yum, yum, that cream should be in my tum!" sang Kissy as she pulled the cloth a bit more. Suddenly, the cream jug and jam pot fell to the floor with a crash!

"Oh, Kissy!" shrieked Winnie. "What have you done?"

Jam and cream went everywhere – what a mess! Kissy Kitten could hardly speak for laughing. "Oh, Winnie," she giggled. "That was so funny!"

Mummy Cat threw her paws in the air, when she saw the mess. "Goodness me," she said. "How could you let Kissy get so sticky, Winnie Kitten? Now I shall have to wash you both!"

Kissy giggled, as Mummy Cat licked her clean. "Bibble and bat, I like that!" she sang.

But Winnie wasn't happy at all. "Ow! Miaow!" she cried, as Mummy Cat's tongue lapped up the jam.

Kissy loved playing with Ginger because Ginger liked to pretend he was a fierce tiger, hunting wild animals or pouncing on Mummy Cat's twitching tail. Today, they were both hunting a Monster Mouse in the vegetable patch. "There's a dangerous mud puddle over there, Kissy," whispered Ginger. "Whatever you do, don't go in it!"

"Fiddle, fuddle, who cares for a puddle?" sang Kissy as she crawled right through the sticky, squelchy mud. Her beautiful white coat got muddier and muddier. She looked as if she was wearing brown boots!

Ginger hid his eyes. "I can't look!" he said. Kissy laughed and laughed. Then, she shook the mud off her dainty paws – all over Ginger!

Mummy Cat howled when she saw her two dirty kittens. "Ginger Kitten! How could you have let Kissy get so muddy?" she cried. "It will take me ages to clean you both!"

"Piddle and pud, that feels good!" sang Kissy.

Poor Ginger didn't feel good at all. "Ow! Miaow!" he wailed, as Mummy Cat cleaned up his coat.

Mummy Cat looked at her kittens and shook her head. "I just can't understand it," she said. "You've always been such good kittens!" Timmy, Winnie and Ginger all frowned at Kissy, who was fast asleep, purring in their basket.

"It wasn't us!" they cried. "We told Kissy Kitten to be careful! We don't like being bathed!" cried the kittens. "We don't like getting soaked or covered with sticky stuff or coated with mud!"

Mummy Cat looked into the basket. "Kissy?" she said. Kissy opened a bright, green eye and said, "But Mummy, I just love it when you kiss my nose and wash me every time I get messy!"

"What a funny Kissy Kitten you are!" said Mummy Cat, giving her a big lick. "You can have a kiss any time you want. You don't have to get really messy first!"

"No, we'd prefer it if you didn't!" said Timmy.

"But we forgive you," said Winnie and Ginger.

Kissy promised never to get them messy again. Then, they all cuddled up together in their basket and went fast asleep!

Town Mouse and Country Mouse

Once there was a roly-poly, wiggly-whiskered mouse, who lived in a snug little nest under an oak tree. Country Mouse loved his home. He had plenty of acorns, nuts and berries to eat and a warm and cosy straw bed to sleep in. Squirrel and Robin, who lived in the oak tree, were the best neighbours he could ever wish for.

One day, Country Mouse had a surprise. His cousin, Town Mouse, came to visit from the Big City. Town Mouse was sleek and slender, with a smooth, shiny coat. His whiskers were smart and elegant. Country Mouse felt a little ordinary beside him. But he didn't mind. All he wanted to do was make Town Mouse feel welcome. "Are you hungry, Cousin?" he said. "Come and have some supper!"

But Town Mouse didn't like the acorns and blackberries that Country Mouse gave him to eat. They were tough and sour. And Town Mouse thought his cousin's friends were boring. The straw bed that he slept in that night was so rough and scratchy that he didn't sleep a wink!

Next day, Town Mouse said, "Come to the Big City with me, Cousin. It's so much more exciting than the country! I live in a grand house, eat delicious food and have exciting adventures. Come with me and see what you've been missing!" It sounded so wonderful, Country Mouse couldn't resist it. Saying goodbye to his friends, the cousins set off for the city.

When they arrived in the Big City, Country Mouse was frightened. It was so noisy – horns blared and wheels clattered all around them. Huge lorries roared and rumbled down the street and the smelly, smoky air made them choke and cough. And there were dogs *everywhere*!

At last, they arrived safely at Town Mouse's house. It was very grand, just as Town Mouse had said. But it was *so* big! Country Mouse was afraid that he would get lost!

"Don't worry," said Town Mouse to Country Mouse. "You'll soon learn your way around the house. For now, just stay close to me. I'm starving – let's go and have a snack." Country Mouse was hungry, too, so he followed his cousin to the kitchen.

Country Mouse had never seen so much delicious food – there were plates full of fruit, nuts, cheese and cakes.

179

He and his cousin ate and ate and ate! But Country Mouse wasn't used to this sort of rich food. Before he knew it, his tummy was aching.

Suddenly, a huge woman came into the room. "Eek! Mice!" she screamed. She grabbed a big broom and began to swat the mice, who scampered off as fast as they could.

As the two mice scurried across the floor, Country Mouse thought things couldn't possibly get worse. But how wrong he was! A big cat suddenly sprang out from behind a chair! With a loud "MEEOOWW," he pounced on the two little mice. Country Mouse had never been so frightened. He darted and dashed as fast as his aching tummy would let him. The two mice jumped through a mousehole and were safe at last in Town Mouse's house.

"Phew! I think we've done enough for one day," said Town

Mouse, when they had caught their breath.
"Let's get some sleep," he said, with a yawn.
"I'll show you the rest of the house in the morning."
Country Mouse curled up in the hard little bed. But he
was too frightened and unhappy to sleep. As he listened
to his cousin snore, he tried hard not
to cry.

Next morning, Town
Mouse was ready for more
adventures, but Country Mouse
had had more than enough.
"Thank you for inviting me," he told
his cousin, "but I have seen all I want to see
of the Big City. It is too big and noisy and dirty – and too
full of danger for me. I want to go back to my quiet,
peaceful home in the country."

So, Country Mouse went back to his
snug, cosy home under the
oak tree. He had never
been so happy to see
his friends – and
they wanted to
hear all about
his adventures.
Country Mouse was
pleased to tell them
everything that had
happened in the
Big City – but he
never, ever went
back there again!

Pigs will be Pigs

Everyone on Old MacDonald's farm knew that it would soon be Old George's birthday. The horse had reached a great age – most of the animals couldn't even count that high!

"We must organise a special party with lots of games," Maria the sheep whispered.

"That would be fun for us," said Poppy the cow, "but George is a very old horse. I don't think he'd like it that much."

Now, a pig's mind is never far from food, so it was not surprising when Percy suggested that they have a feast! "If we all keep some of our food back each day, we'll have lots saved up by George's birthday!" he said.

Everyone agreed that a feast was a good idea. The animals found a place at the back of the barn to hide the food – well away from Old MacDonald's prying eyes!

Soon, they had a huge pile of the most tasty, delicious and scrummy things ready for the party – and they were all getting very excited as the day drew nearer.

The evening before the feast, the pile of food was massive! The animals knew that Mr and Mrs MacDonald would be going to market early the next morning – they would have the whole farmyard all to themselves.

As night fell, some of the little animals were too excited to sleep.

As the moon rose over Old MacDonald's farm, Percy found himself wide awake. He tossed and turned, and turned and tossed, trying very hard not to think about the piles of delicious food.

Now, there is nothing that makes a pig so hungry as knowing that there are good things to eat nearby. Even though he knew that the food was meant for the party, and no matter how hard he tried, Percy simply could not forget that food.

"Just a mouthful or two wouldn't matter," he said to himself. "No one would miss the odd juicy apple, or a handful of corn, would they?" Percy's mouth began to water.

Percy crept out of his sty, walking on trotter tiptoes. He reached the door of the barn. Creeeaaaaaak! He pushed it open with his nose and went inside.

"GOT YOU, PERCY PIG!" clucked Jenny the hen, jumping up from behind a bale of straw. "Percy, old thing," she grinned, "we knew you wouldn't be able to resist all this gorgeous food, so we've been on guard all week. Go straight back to bed and wait until morning." Percy blushed – he had been caught out!

184

The next morning, as all the animals tucked in to the fabulous feast, Percy told the others that he was sorry.

"Never you mind," they said. "Pigs will be pigs! Here, have another apple, Percy!"

A Goodnight Kiss

"It's bedtime now, Oakey," said Mum. Oakey curled up in the chair. His ears began to droop and he muttered, "Oh, that's not fair!"

"Have a drink first," smiled Mum, "then you must go."

"Five minutes more!" begged Oakey.

Mum answered, "No!"

Oakey's ears drooped and off he went. But he was back in a flash! "Where's your drink?" asked Mum. "You haven't been very long. You look scared, Oakey. Is there something wrong?"

"There's a monster in the kitchen, with long, white shaggy hair, lurking in the corner, behind the rocking chair," said Oakey.

Mum laughed. "Oh, Oakey, you've made a mistake. That's no monster. It's a mop." And she gave the mop a shake.

Oakey's ears drooped and off he went. But he was back in a flash! "What's the matter?" asked Mum.

"There's a ghost in the hallway, hovering around. Look, there it is floating just above the ground," he wailed.

"Oh, Oakey, you've made a mistake. That's no ghost. It's just an old coat, hanging on the hook. Coats don't float!" laughed Mum.

Oakey's ears drooped and off he went. But he was back in a flash! "Why aren't you in bed, Oakey?" asked Mum.

"There's a great big lump beneath the sheets. It's waiting to get me. I'm scared it's going to pounce. Please come and see," sniffed Oakey.

"Oh, Oakey, you've made a mistake. The only thing underneath the sheets is your old teddy bear," smiled Mum.

Oakey's ears drooped and he got into bed. But he didn't close his eyes. "Why aren't you asleep?" asked Mum.

"There are huge creepy crawlies underneath my bed. And I can't get the thought of them out of my head," complained Oakey.

"They're just your slippers, Oakey, so there's no need to hide. They won't be creeping anywhere without your feet inside," grinned Mum. "That's it now, Oakey. Time to say goodnight."

Mum left the room, switching off the light. And then Oakey saw it by the door. The monster! It moved across the floor and walked straight towards him, with its arms stretched out. Oakey's mouth opened, but he found he couldn't shout. The monster leaned over him and Oakey closed his eyes. What happened next gave Oakey an enormous surprise. The monster picked him up and cuddled him tight. Monsters just don't do that.

This couldn't be right! Then Mum's voice whispered, "Don't worry, it's just me. When I said 'Goodnight' just now, I forgot to give you this." Then Monster Mum gave Oakey a goodnight kiss!

I Wish...

I wonder what you would be if you weren't you. I like to sit and think of all the things I would like to be...

Sometimes I wish I was an elephant because it would make me laugh to sit in the bath and use my nose as a hose to rinse off all my bubbles.

Or I wish I was a chameleon because then I could change the colour of my skin to hide anywhere, and no one would be able to see me!

If I was a hippo I would be able to mess about all day and get as dirty as I liked, and no one would tell me off.

Or if I could be a dolphin I would be able to leap and splash about in the water having fun all day, and swim with the fish.

I suppose I could be an ostrich, but I am not sure that if I was frightened I would really want to hide my head in the sand!

I think that I will stay as me – but I won't stop wondering about being something else!

Index